"Why Would You Want To Help Me? You Don't Even Know Me."

Mack kept his gaze fixed on hers. "I know more than you might think. I know that the father of your baby isn't going to be around to take care of you or the child."

Addy's jaw dropped, then closed with an angry click of teeth. "You don't know any such thing."

"Yes, I do," he replied calmly. "If his past actions are any indication, you'll never hear from Ty again."

Her eyes widened. "You—you know Ty?"

"He's my half brother."

"You mean, you knew about me and the baby before—"

"Yes, that's why I dropped by your house. I was there to offer you money."

Steam all but came out of her ears. "Well, you can tell Ty to keep his damn money. I don't want it."

"The money's not Ty's. It's mine."

"Well, I don't want your money, either, Mack McGruder." She pointed a stiff finger at the door. "Get out. And don't bother coming back."

Dear Reader,

Who can resist a baby? With their sweet, cherub faces and tiny, little fingers and toes, a baby can melt even the hardest of hearts. Recently our niece blessed my husband and I with a great-nephew, Charlie Corbell. Charlie's birth was truly a miracle, as he was born very premature. Thanks to the dedicated staff of doctors and nurses who supervised his care, I'm happy to report that Charlie is healthy as a horse and growing like a weed.

A birth spawns a variety of emotions within those touched by the process: pride and joy for the mother and father; satisfaction for the nurses and doctors. Sometimes even a complete stranger is affected by a birth, as is the case with Mack McGruder, the hero in this story.

I hope you enjoy reading Mack and Addy's story, and share the joy in the birth of Addy's son.

Peggy Moreland

PEGGY MORELAND

The Texan's Convenient Marriage

Published by Silhouette Books
America's Publisher of Contemporary Romance

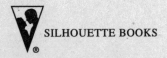 SILHOUETTE BOOKS

ISBN-13: 978-0-373-76736-6
ISBN-10:   0-373-76736-6

THE TEXAN'S CONVENIENT MARRIAGE

Copyright © 2006 by Peggy Bozeman Morse

Visit Silhouette Books at www.eHarlequin.com

Printed in U.S.A.

Books by Peggy Moreland

PEGGY MORELAND

published her first romance with Silhouette in 1989, and continues to delight readers with stories set in her home state of Texas. Winner of the National Readers' Choice Award, a nominee for *Romantic Times BOOKclub* Reviewer's Choice Award and a two-time finalist for the prestigious RITA® Award, Peggy's books frequently appear on the *USA Today* and Waldenbooks bestseller lists. When not writing, you can usually find Peggy outside, tending the cattle, goats and other critters on the ranch she shares with her husband. You may write to Peggy at P.O. Box 1099, Florence, TX 76527-1099, or e-mail her at peggy@peggymoreland.com.

To my daughter, Hilary. Thanks for your willingness to read my work, your encouragement when I need it most and for the smile you put in my heart.

Prologue

War is fear cloaked in courage.
—William Westmoreland

Smoke hung in the air cloaking the darkness, its acrid scent burning the noses of the soldiers hiding in the tall grass. Some had taken advantage of the lull in activity and had stretched out, eyes closed, their guns held at the ready across their chests, their packs pillowed beneath their heads. Others were hunkered down, watching…and waiting.

Antonio Rocci, or Romeo as he was called by his friends, wanted to sleep but couldn't. Fear kept his eyes open and his ears cocked for any sound of movement in the inky darkness. In the distance, red embers and thin curls of smoke marked where a small village had once stood. Reconnaissance had reported that Vietcong soldiers had infiltrated the village and were using the area to store artillery. Earlier that day, while the sun was still up, an air attack had taken place. Constructed mainly of grasses and bamboo gathered from the surrounding countryside, the hooches that had once formed the small village had gone up like dry kindling. All that remained were burning embers and the cloying smell of smoke.

When morning came, it was the job of Romeo and the other soldiers in his unit to go into the village and search for the cache of artillery and ammunition reportedly hidden there. A side duty was checking for survivors and counting the dead. Bile rose in Romeo's throat at the thought of what he might face, and he quickly swallowed it down. It's war, he reminded himself. It's either us or them, and he'd a hell of a lot rather it be them.

"Romeo?"

He jumped at the voice, then forced the tension from his body when he realized it was Pops, their team leader, who had spoken.

He set his jaw to steady his voice, hide the fear. "Over here."

He heard a slight rustle of grass, and angled his head, watching as Pop's shadowed form moved closer.

"You okay?" Pops whispered.

Romeo released his grip on his gun long enough to drag his arm across the nervous perspiration that beaded his forehead, then settled his finger over the trigger again. "Yeah, but I'd feel a whole lot better if I knew we were the only ones out here."

"Yeah," Pops agreed soberly. "I hear you."

Silence settled between them, as both continued to watch the darkness.

Romeo would never admit it, but he felt safer, less vulnerable with Pops at his side. Older than most of the others in the unit, Pops—the nickname given to Larry Blair by the rest of the team—had already completed one tour of duty in Vietnam and was working on his second. Romeo couldn't imagine why anyone would willingly sign on for another tour. From the day he'd arrived in country, he'd felt as if he'd been dropped down into the bowels of hell and couldn't wait for the day he could board the plane that would carry him home.

"Pops?"

"Yeah?"

"Do you ever regret signing on for a second tour?"

"No sense regretting what you can't change."

Romeo angled his head to peer at the man whose opinion he respected as much as he would his father's. "Do you ever get scared, Pops?"

"Yeah," Pops admitted quietly. "It's the soldier who fears nothing that gets himself killed. If you use fear to your advantage, it'll keep you alert, on guard, prepared. Give in to it and it'll make you helpless, weak."

Romeo considered that for a moment, but found little comfort in Pop's advice. He'd always considered himself brave, even cocky. Now he wondered if he had a bright-yellow stripe running down his back.

"Is being afraid the same as being a coward?" he asked hesitantly.

"No. A coward runs and hides."

"Some of the guys think Preacher's a coward."

"Well, they're wrong. Preacher just can't bear the thought of taking a human life. It's his beliefs he struggles with, not cowardice."

Romeo considered that a moment, then shook his head sadly. "Hell, it doesn't matter if you're a hero or a coward. We all die just the same."

Pop pulled a package of gum from his pocket. "Don't think about dying," he warned, and offered a piece to Romeo. He unwrapped one for himself and folded the strip of gum in two, before popping it into his mouth. "Think about living, about what you're going to do when you get home."

Romeo gulped, thinking about what he'd left behind, what would be waiting for him when he returned. "Have I ever told you why I joined the service?"

"Can't say as you have."

"I got a girl pregnant."

He felt Pop's gaze and, for once, was grateful for the darkness so that Pop couldn't see his face, his shame. "She was putting pressure on me to marry her. I figured the army was as good a way to get out of it, as any."

If Pop had an opinion, he kept it to himself, which Romeo appreciated. He wasn't looking for absolution…or a lecture. What he wanted was a sounding board, someone who would listen.

"It was wrong," he admitted with regret. "Running

away, I mean. Even if I didn't want to marry her, I should've at least agreed to share responsibility for the kid. It's mine, a part of me. I shouldn't have left her to deal with it alone." He glanced over at Pops. "Do you think it's too late?"

Pop frowned in confusion. "For what?"

"To provide for the kid. I was thinking maybe I could send her some money."

"I'm sure she'd appreciate it," Pop replied.

"Yeah," Romeo said, warming to the idea. "And when I get home and get a real job, I could send her a set amount every month. Kinda like the child support my dad had to pay my mom after they divorced."

"Sounds fair," Pops agreed. "A man should take care of what's his."

Romeo frowned, as a new thought rose. "But what happens if I don't make it home?" He glanced over at Pops. "Who'll take care of my kid then?"

Pops clasped Romeo's shoulder, gave it a squeeze. "Don't talk like that. You're going to make it home. We all are."

Though Romeo appreciated the reassurance, he knew Pops was blowing smoke. There were no guarantees. Not for any of them. And if he did get killed, what would happen to the baby he'd fathered? He didn't have anything of value to leave behind. No savings, no property. Hell, he didn't even own a car. He'd sold his old heap to his cousin, before he'd left for 'Nam.

"Pops?"

"Yeah?"

"Remember the deed that rancher tore up and gave to us the day before we shipped out?"

"Yeah. What about it?"

"The old man said he was going to give us his ranch when we got home. My portion of the deed is in my footlocker back at camp. If something happens to me, would you see that my kid gets it?"

"Nothing's going to happen to you," Pop maintained stubbornly.

"But if something does, promise me you'll send it to Mary Claire Richards. Tell her it's for the baby."

There was a long pause of silence, before Pop said quietly, "Consider it done."

One

Addy pressed the heel of her hand against the ache building between her eyes. Another five minutes on the phone with her mother and it would surpass the one that had throbbed low in her back all day.

Drawing in a deep breath, she searched for patience.

"I know you don't like to talk about my father," she began, choosing her words carefully. "But this is important. A lady called. Stephanie Parker. She said her father served with mine in Vietnam."

"So what if he did?" her mother snapped. "Thousands of American soldiers went to Vietnam."

Ignoring her mother's bitterness, Addy forged on, determined to get through this conversation without screaming. "Stephanie told me that her father sent her mother a letter from Vietnam with a torn piece of paper inside. She thinks Tony might have had a similar piece and sent it to you."

"The only thing Antonio Rocci ever gave me was *you* and that was an accident."

Addy didn't flinch at the jab at her illegitimacy. She'd had the circumstances surrounding her birth thrown in her face so often over the years that hearing it no longer had the power to sting.

"This paper may be valuable," she persisted. "Do you remember Tony sending you anything like that?"

"That was over thirty years ago! How am I supposed to remember something that happened that long ago? I don't even remember what was in yesterday's mail."

"A torn piece of paper, Mom. That's odd enough that you should remember."

"If you called to talk about *him*, I'm hanging up. I'm missing my shows."

Before Addy could say anything more, the dial tone buzzed in her ear.

"The baby and I are doing fine, but thanks for asking."

Scowling, she slammed down the phone, furious with herself for letting her mother's lack of concern get to her. Mary Claire Richards-Smith-Carlton-Sullivan was a neurotic, self-centered woman who raced from one bad marriage to the next, fueled by a bitterness she'd clung to for more than thirty years and oblivious to anyone else's needs, including her daughter's.

With a sigh Addy swept a stray lock of hair from her face and told herself it didn't matter. She'd survived thirty-three years of her mother's disregard. Why should she expect her to show any concern now?

She stooped to untie her shoelaces but froze when she caught a glimpse of her reflection on the patio door. Straightening slowly, she stared, barely recognizing the woman who stared back. Her stomach looked as if she'd swallowed a soccer ball, her feet and ankles so swollen they looked like an elephant's, and her long, black hair—which she usually considered her best feature— was wadded up in a frizzy knot on top of her head. Add to that lovely image nurses' scrubs in a putrid shade of green and a well-worn pair of Reeboks and she was almost glad Ty wasn't around to see her now.

Grimacing, she reached to untie her shoelaces again. "As if I'd let him past the front door," she muttered under her breath. Ty Bodean was a lying snake and she was better off without him, even if it did mean she'd be raising her baby alone.

She caught her lower lip between her teeth as she eased the shoe off her swollen foot, thinking what all that meant, what lay ahead of her. Money was going to be a problem. Eighteen months ago, she'd bought the house, which had depleted her savings and shackled her to a mortgage payment that already stretched her monthly budget to the limit. At the time she'd made the purchase, it had seemed a wise investment. She'd always wanted to have her own home, and the previous owner had offered it to her at a ridiculously low price. Of course, when she'd agreed to buy the property, she hadn't been pregnant and had no plans of becoming pregnant in the near future. An unforgettable—albeit brief—affair with Ty Bodean had changed all that.

The second problem—which was tied directly to the first—was child care. She hated the thought of her baby being raised by strangers, but as the major and *only* breadwinner in the family, there was no way she could quit her job and stay at home with her baby.

The third problem was raising a child in a single-parent home. Again she had no other option, but she was determined to do a better job of it than her own mother had done in raising her.

The reminder of her mother sent her thoughts segueing to the father she'd never known and the phone call she'd received concerning him. She frowned thoughtfully as she considered the torn piece of paper Stephanie Parker had mentioned.

Could it really be valuable? she asked herself, then sputtered a laugh. Even if it was, which she seriously doubted, she couldn't cash in on something she couldn't find. She supposed she could paw her way through the trunk her mother had left in her garage for safekeeping. If it was anywhere, it would be there.

But not tonight, she thought, heaving a weary sigh. She'd put in a long, back-breaking eight-hour shift in Emergency, and she wasn't doing anything more strenuous that evening than propping up her feet and watching TV.

Bracing a hand against the counter for support, she lifted her foot to tug off her remaining shoe. As she did, a pain knifed through her midsection, stealing her breath. Eyes wide, she hugged an arm around her middle and sank slowly to her knees. With a hand propped on the floor to keep herself upright, she forced herself to take slow, even breaths, and tried to think of a logical explanation for the pain. It couldn't be labor, she told herself. Her due date was still almost two months away. It had to be Braxton Hicks, she decided. False labor. She'd experienced similar pains before. None as severe as this, but she knew it would soon pass, just as the others had.

But as she knelt, waiting for the pain to lessen, it grew stronger, more intense, as if a vise had been clamped around her middle and cinched up tight. Sweat broke out on her brow, beading her upper lip. She couldn't move, could barely breathe. She glanced up at the counter and the phone just out of reach, and gulped back the nausea, the fear, knowing she had to call for help. But who? She hated to call 911, if this turned out to be false labor. She worked in Emergency. She knew how much manpower and time was wasted on expectant mothers who were convinced they were in labor.

She'd call her neighbor, she decided. Mrs. Baker would stay with her until she could determine that this was the real thing and not a false alarm.

As she lifted a hand to the counter to pull herself up, another pain, nearly blinding in its intensity, dragged her back down to her knees. Moaning, she curled into a ball, trying to smother the pain. She felt a gush of moisture between her legs and watched in horror as a dark stain spread from the crotch of her scrub pants, soaking her to the knees.

She squeezed her eyes shut against the sight, knowing all too well what this meant.

"Oh, God, please," she prayed tearfully. "Don't let me lose my baby."

Mack climbed from his car and checked the number on the house against the return address on the envelope he held, then tucked it into his shirt pocket and studied the house. Its modest appearance and old-fashioned charm surprised him. Similar trips in the past had taken him to ultramodern condominiums in singles' neighborhoods and upscale apartment high-rises, but nothing even close to this. This house seemed almost…well, homey. From the border of impatiens that lined the sidewalk, to the baskets of ferns that swung lazily from hooks on the porch eaves, it looked like a place where a family might live.

Reminded that it was his own family who was responsible for him being here, he swore under his breath and started up the walk, anxious to get the unsavory task over with. Reaching the door, he rapped his knuckles against wood painted a warm, cheerful red, then rocked back on his boot heels and waited.

After a full minute passed without a response, he lifted a hand and knocked again. Frowning, he strained to listen for any sound coming from inside that would indicate that someone was home. He heard a female voice call out, but wasn't sure what was said. An invitation to come in, he wondered, or simply a signal to let him know she was on her way to the door?

Figuring it was the latter, he waited, listening for the sound of footsteps from inside. When he heard nothing but silence, he tried the door and found it locked. Frowning, he glanced to his left and noticed a set of windows. Though covered by blinds, he crossed to peer through them, hoping they would offer him a peek inside. A narrow gap between the slats provided him with a slim view of the living room. Finding no sign of life, he shifted his gaze to a hallway beyond that led toward the rear of the house. A flutter of movement on the floor caught his attention and he pressed his nose against the glass for a better look.

"What the hell," he murmured, as he stared at what appeared to be an outstretched hand, its fingers clawing against the hardwood floor. Was the woman drunk and had fallen? he wondered. Had she OD'd? Either possibility wouldn't surprise him, considering the crowd Ty ran with. But it was the other possibilities that came to mind—attempted burglary, possible rape victim—that had him leaping off the porch and running around to the rear of the house. His heart thumping wildly, he cleared the back porch steps in one leap and shoved open the door.

Braced for a possible attack, he stepped cautiously inside. "Ma'am?" he called. "Are you okay?"

"Help me…please."

The voice, weak and thready, came from the opposite side of the room.

He quickly rounded the island that separated the

room and found the woman lying on the floor, her back to him. From her sprawled position, it appeared she had heard his knock and had tried to drag herself to the front door.

He dropped to a knee behind her and laid a hand on her arm. "Are you hurt?"

"I—"

Moaning, she curled tighter into herself.

"My…water…broke," she managed to gasp out between breaths.

A chill skated down Mack's spine. He had known the woman was pregnant but hadn't realized she was that far along. "How far apart are the contractions?"

She dragged in a breath, slowly released it, then rolled to her back and looked up at him.

"Continuous." She wet her lips. "Please…help me." Tears welled up in her eyes and spilled over dark lashes. "I don't want to lose my baby."

He set his jaw against the fear in her eyes, the desperation in her voice. He didn't need this nightmare, he told himself. He could walk out the door right now, tear up the check he'd brought along to end whatever responsibility the woman felt his family owed her, and no one would ever be the wiser.

Her hand closed over his, her fingers digging deeply into his skin. "Please," she begged. "You've got to help me."

He hesitated a moment, then swore under his breath and pushed to his feet. With his mouth slanted in a scowl, he snatched the phone from its base and punched in 911.

* * *

Mack paced the waiting area of the Emergency Room, his stomach in knots, his palms slick with sweat. His uneasiness wasn't due to his concern for the woman who had been wheeled away by EMS thirty minutes earlier. It was the hospital. He hated them. The antiseptic smell. The sterile decor. The constant pages over the PA system for doctors and nurses and the dreaded words "code blue." He didn't know what had possessed him to come here. He'd done what the woman had asked of him. He'd called 911, then stayed with her until the ambulance arrived. He'd done his duty. If she lost her baby, it was no skin off his nose. It wasn't his kid.

He dropped his head back with a groan, unable to believe that he would even think such a thing. He didn't wish the woman ill. And he sure as hell didn't want her to lose her baby. He knew what it was like to lose a child. The grief, the guilt, the hole it left in your heart, in your life.

"Mr. McGruder?"

He whirled at the sound of his name and found a nurse standing in the doorway. "Yes?"

"Ms. Rocci is asking for you." She opened the door wider. "If you'll follow me, I'll show you the way."

He hesitated, knowing it was a mistake to see the woman again, to get involved any deeper than he already was. He should leave. Go back home where he belonged. Forget about Adrianna Rocci and her unborn child.

Instead he found himself following the nurse down a long hall.

She glanced over her shoulder. "You're a bit of a hero around here, you know."

He frowned, uncomfortable at being tagged as such. "I'm no hero."

"You are to us. You came to the aid of one of our own." At his confused looked, she explained. "Addy works here. If you hadn't happened along when you did, there's a chance she would've lost her baby. Maybe even her life."

Before he could think of a response, she stopped before one of the curtained-off cubicles, pushed back the drape and held it aside.

When he hesitated, she gave him a reassuring smile. "Don't worry," she whispered. "She's resting more comfortably now."

Taking a deep breath, he stepped inside. The room was so small the curtain brushed the backs of his legs when the nurse dropped it into place. The woman— Addy, he remembered the nurse calling her—lay on a gurney parked no more than a foot from where he stood, a sheet draping her from chin to toes. A white identification bracelet circled her left wrist and an IV needle was taped to the back of her hand. He followed the tube to a bottle hooked to a stainless steel pole wheeled close to the bed, then shifted his gaze to her face.

With her eyes closed and her hands folded over her swollen stomach, she looked serene, peaceful. Thinking she was asleep, he eased closer to the bed and was relieved to find that there was more color in her face than there had been when the attendants had loaded her into the ambulance.

She wasn't beautiful, he thought as he studied her, but she wasn't homely, either. Her complexion was dark, as was her hair, a testament to her Italian surname, he supposed. Her cheekbones were high ridges, her neck long and graceful.

As he stared, trying to remember the color of her eyes, her lashes fluttered up. Brown, he noted. Her eyes were brown.

She smiled softly and reached for his hand. "I can't believe you're really here. I was sure that I had imagined you."

Her voice was husky, barely more than a whisper, but he heard the wonder in it. "The nurse said you wanted to see me."

She gave his hand a grateful squeeze. "To thank you." She closed her eyes, gulped. When she opened them again, a single tear slipped from the corner and slid down her temple to disappear into her hair. "I don't know what would've happened to me and my baby if you hadn't come along when you did."

He averted his gaze, unsure what to say. When he glanced back, she was studying him curiously, as if only just now wondering at his identity and why he was at her house.

"Do I know you?"

He hesitated a moment, then figured she'd never make the connection. "John McGruder, though most folks call me Mack."

"Mack," she repeated, as if testing the sound of the name, then smiled. "That's a good, strong name. It suits you."

Before he could think of a response, her eyes slammed shut and she arched up high off the bed, her fingers digging into the mattress.

Panicking, he glanced around for a call button. "Should I get the nurse?"

She released a long breath, then opened her eyes and forced a reassuring smile. "No. I'm okay. The doctor was able to stop the labor, but he said I should expect a few more pains."

He blew out a long breath of his own, relieved that it hadn't lasted any longer than it had. "Does that mean you get to go home?"

"No. In fact, an orderly is on his way right now to take me up to Labor and Delivery."

"But I thought you said the doctor was able to stop your labor?"

"He was…for the time being. But I have to stay in the hospital. They need to be able to monitor the baby's vital signs, plus keep me off my feet."

"How long will you have to stay?"

She lifted a shoulder. "Until the baby's born. My actual due date isn't until July 15, but Dr. Wharton says he doubts I'll make it that long."

He did the math in his head and shuddered, knowing he'd go nuts if he had to stay in a hospital bed for six weeks. "Is there anyone I can call for you? Family you want notified?"

She shook her head. "The only family I have is my mother, and she lives in Hawaii."

He pulled a pen from his pocket. "Give me her number, and I'll give her a call. She'll probably want to catch the next plane out."

"You're sweet to offer, but it isn't necessary. She wasn't planning on coming for the baby's birth. Me going into labor early won't change her mind."

He pressed the pen against the paper. "Why don't you let her decide that?"

She hesitated a moment, then sighed. "I guess it wouldn't hurt to let her know what's going on. Her name is Mary Claire Sullivan and her number is—"

Mack jotted down the number she rattled off, then slipped the paper and pen back into his pocket. He glanced uncertainly around. "Well, I guess I better get out of here before they run me off. Is there anything I can get for you before I leave?"

She lifted a brow. "About six more weeks of pregnancy?" Smiling, she flapped a hand. "Just kidding. I'll be fine."

He shifted uneasily from foot to foot, anxious to go, but reluctant to leave her alone. "You take care of yourself, okay?"

She reached for his hand and gave it another grateful squeeze. "Thanks, Mack. For everything. I owe you one."

As Mack stepped through the Emergency Room doors, he pulled his cell phone from the holster clipped at his waist and punched in the number Addy had given him, wanting to make the call to her mother before he hit the road.

When a woman answered, he asked, "Is this Mary Claire Sullivan?"

"Who wants to know?"

Mack scowled at the woman's suspicious tone. "Mack McGruder. I'm calling for your daughter. Addy," he added, thinking she might have more than one. "She went into labor earlier this evening and was rushed to the hospital. The doctor was able to stop the labor, but she's going to have to remain in the hospital until the baby is born."

"Are you the one who got her pregnant?"

Startled by the unexpected question, he gaped, then scowled again. "No. I'm just passing on information. Figured you'd want to make arrangements to come and stay with her."

"If she thinks I'm going to fly all the way to Dallas to hold her hand, she's got another think coming! Nobody sat by my side while I was giving birth to her. No siree. I sweated out twelve hours of labor all by myself. Twelve *long* hours," she added. "And even if I wanted to come, which I don't, I've got a husband to see after. I can't go flying off and leave him to fend for himself. You tell Addy that she's the one who got herself into this mess, and she'll have to see it to its end. I've got troubles enough of my own to deal with, without taking on hers."

Stunned, Mack stood slack-jawed. How could a mother be so callous about her own child? So uncaring?

"If it's the cost you're worried about, I'll arrange for your flight."

"A man who'd offer to do that either has a guilty conscience or money to burn."

Mack ground his teeth. "I'm just trying to be helpful. I'd think you'd want to be with your daughter at a time like this."

"She got pregnant without my help. She can deliver without it, too."

"But she's your daughter!" he shouted, unable to contain his frustration any longer. "She needs you."

"I did my duty by Addy. I raised her, didn't I? And without any help from the sorry SOB who fathered her."

Mack wanted to curse at the woman, strangle something, preferably her. How could anyone, much less a mother, be so cold-blooded?

"I'm sorry I bothered you," he muttered, and disconnected the call before he gave in to the urge to tell the woman exactly what he thought of her. Scowling, he stuffed his cell phone back into its holster at his waist, then dragged his hands over his hair. Lacing his fingers behind his head, he glanced over his shoulder at the Emergency Room door and envisioned Addy lying on the gurney, probably worried out of her mind about her baby, and without a soul to lean on for support.

Dropping his arms, he headed for the parking lot, telling himself it wasn't his problem. He'd done his duty. He'd called the ambulance for her, made sure that she'd arrived safely at the hospital. He'd even called her mother for her.

He did an abrupt about-face and marched back to the Emergency entrance. Once inside, he quickly spotted the nurse who had taken him back to see Addy and motioned her toward him.

"Leaving us?" she asked, smiling.

"Yes, ma'am. I've got a good four-hour drive home." He fished a business card from his wallet and handed it to her. "I'd appreciate it if you'd give me a call if there's a change in Addy's condition. My cell number is there at the bottom. Call day or night. Doesn't matter. I'll answer."

She hid a smile. "And you claimed you're not a hero," she scolded.

"More like a janitor," he grumbled, and turned for the door.

"Janitor?" she repeated in confusion.

He paused in the open doorway and glanced back. "Yeah. Seems I've made a career of cleaning up other people's messes."

Two

Addy thrust her head back against the pillow and clenched her teeth, sure that the pain was going to rip her apart. In spite of her efforts to suppress it, a low animal-like groan slid past her lips, and she began to pant, determined to stay ahead of the pain and not give in to it.

Busy adjusting an intravenous drip, Marjorie glanced her way. "Bad?"

Gulping, Addy nodded. "Did you call Dr. Wharton?"

Satisfied that the fluids were transferring at the proper rate, Marjorie took Addy's hand and held it between her own. "He's on his way."

Addy gulped again. "He better hurry."

Her expression sympathetic, Marjorie stroked Addy's

damp hair back from her face. "I know you don't want to hear this, but you're a long way from delivering."

Groaning, Addy closed her eyes. "I can't be. The pain is already unbearable." She opened her eyes and looked at Marjorie, tears blurring her friend's image. "You'd tell me if something was wrong with the baby, wouldn't you?"

"Of course I would," Marjorie assured her.

Addy searched her friend's face, trying to determine if she was telling the truth or just saying that to keep Addy from becoming more upset. Unsure, she looked away. "You should go back down to Emergency. You're on duty."

Marjorie glanced toward the door and worried her lip. "I really should. There was a bus wreck on the interstate. The call came in just before I came up to check on you."

Addy pulled her hand from Marjorie's. "Then go. They need you more than I do."

"But I hate leaving you alone," Marjorie fretted.

"I'll be okay. Really."

"I'll call Mack," Marjorie said, already digging in her pocket for her cell phone. "He gave me his number and said for me to let him know if there was a change in your condition."

"No, please," Addy begged. "He's done enough for me already. Promise you won't call him."

Marjorie eyed Addy stubbornly for a moment, then sagged her shoulders in defeat. "Oh, all right," she said, and shoved the phone into her pocket. "I'll come back and check on you again as soon as I can."

"Thanks, Marjorie."

Addy waited until the door closed behind her friend, then covered her face with her hands and gave in to the tears that had threatened since her labor had started again. She couldn't lose her baby, prayed God would keep it safe. She wanted this baby so badly, needed it. In spite of all the sacrifices she would have to make to support and care for it, she wanted this baby to live.

And while she was praying, she added a thanks for Mack's unexpected appearance at her house and the steps he'd taken to protect her baby's life.

Even as the prayer formed, she lowered her hands from her face and frowned, wondering about Mack and realizing that, although she'd asked him his name, she'd failed to ask him why he'd been at her house.

There were any number of plausible explanations, she reminded herself. He could be a bill collector or a solicitor. Her frown deepened. But that didn't make sense, as she didn't have any outstanding bills and solicitors were prohibited in her neighborhood. She supposed he might have become lost and simply stopped to ask directions, which wasn't unusual, as her neighborhood was made up of a tangle of streets that baffled even the most gifted map reader.

Whatever his reason, she thought, dismissing her concerns as unnecessary considering his kindness to her, she wished he was still with her. She knew it was stupid, foolish even, to yearn for someone she didn't even know. But while he'd been with her, both at her house and in Emergency, she'd felt safe, more in control, better capable of handling the pain, of facing whatever happened. Not so alone.

She opened her hands to look at them, remembering how sure his grip had felt on hers, how firmly he'd held her hand. How strong he'd seemed, so in control. He didn't even know her, yet he'd followed the ambulance to the hospital, stayed with her, even offered to call her mother.

Why couldn't she have fallen for a guy like Mack? she asked herself miserably. She bet he wouldn't have stolen from her or lied to her as Ty had done. And he probably wouldn't have run the way Ty had when she'd told him she was pregnant.

Gulping back the regret that crowded her throat, she closed her eyes and willed her body to relax and her mind to clear, knowing she had to keep her thoughts focused so that she could deal with the next pain when it came.

There'd be plenty of time for regrets later.

A thick band of clouds blocked what light the moon might have offered, leaving the interstate a black ribbon that stretched for miles and miles in the darkness. But Mack didn't mind the darkness or the lack of traffic he encountered. In fact, he welcomed it. It gave him time to think.

And Adrianna Rocci—or Addy, as her friend had called her—had given him a lot to think about.

An unplanned pregnancy. An irresponsible boyfriend. A mother who ranked right up there with Joan Crawford on the nurturing scale. And now her baby's life was in jeopardy. How much more could the woman take, before she snapped?

It wasn't right, he told himself. No one should have to go through something like this alone. She should have a husband or, at the very least, family with her to offer emotional and physical support. Hell, the woman was going to be all but tied to a bed for the next six weeks! Who would take care of her house? Get her mail? Pay her bills? Who would sit with her to help pass the time? Hold her hand when she was scared? Stand at her side during the birth?

He narrowed his eyes at the dark highway ahead, wishing he could get his hands on Ty. Castration came to mind as sufficient punishment, but even that seemed too kind. Getting a woman pregnant, then abandoning her… It just wasn't right. Yet that was Ty's style. Hit and run, love 'em and leave 'em, that was his standard modus operandi. In Mack's estimation, Ty was immature, irresponsible and a royal pain in the ass. Unfortunately, women seemed to find him irresistible. And why wouldn't they? he asked himself. Ty was a good-looking man, smooth talking, fun loving. It was in the integrity department that he came up short. Just like his old man.

Mack scowled at the reminder of his stepfather. Jacob Bodean was nothing but a two-bit con artist out trolling for a free ride, when he'd met Mack's mother. Recently widowed and still grieving over the loss of her husband, his mother had been an easy mark for a scumball like Jacob. Playing on her weakened emotional state, within two months Jacob had sweet-talked her into marrying him. Another fourteen months and Ty had been born.

It had taken Mack's mother six years—and the loss of a large chunk of the fortune Mack's father had left her—before she'd figured out that Jacob was only interested in her money and was going through it as fast as he could write checks. It had cost her another chunk of money to get rid of him and to win custody of Ty. Mack often wondered if she wouldn't have been better off washing her hands of them both.

But Ty is blood, he told himself, as his mother had often reminded him and, like it or not, he was now Mack's responsibility. On her deathbed, his mother had made him promise that he would look after his half brother. The trust fund she'd set up for Ty prior to her death, naming Mack as executor, had added a legal obligation to the moral one he'd already assumed.

Both had been stretched mighty thin over the years.

Mack had bailed Ty out of more trouble than he cared to think about and was sick and damn tired of mopping up a grown man's messes. For God's sake, he thought, his anger with his half brother building. Ty was thirty-four years old! It was past time for him to settle down and take care of his own damn mistakes.

Mack drew in a long breath and slowly released it, telling himself that working up a steam over Ty wasn't going to help Addy's situation. And Addy definitely needed help.

He patted his shirt pocket, remembering the check he'd planned to offer her, in hopes of buying Ty's way out of yet another paternity suit, if that's what she'd had in mind. But after finding her lying on the floor already in labor, he hadn't been able to bring himself to broach the subject. How could he, when she was worried sick she might lose her baby?

But he had to do something, he told himself. He couldn't just leave her hanging out there alone. She'd seemed like a nice person, nothing at all like the other women Ty associated with, who had greedily snatched up the money he had offered them. Yet, what options did Mack have other than to offer her money? He sure as hell couldn't force Ty to do the honorable thing and marry the woman and give the baby his name. Even if he could, he certainly wouldn't be doing Addy any favors, saddling her with a man like Ty.

His cell phone rang, and he quickly plucked it from the console, where he'd laid it, and flipped it open. "Mack," he said.

"This is Marjorie Johnson. The nurse from the Emergency Room?"

He tensed at the hesitancy in the woman's voice, knowing the call had to be about Addy. "Has something happened to Addy?"

"Her labor started again. The doctor says he can't stop it this time. I wanted to stay with her, but I'm on duty and don't get off for another five hours."

He glanced at the illuminated clock on the dash and quickly calculated the time. "I can be there in less than two."

"Oh, thank you," she said in relief, then added in a

rush, "But please don't tell her that I called. When I suggested it, she insisted that I not bother you. Said you'd done enough for her already."

He saw an exit sign up ahead, and took it.

"Don't worry. Your secret is safe with me."

Mack headed straight for Labor and Delivery and the room number the attendant at the information desk had given him.

The room he entered was larger than the tiny cubicle he'd left her in during her stay in the ER. There was also more equipment on hand, all of which was humming and blinking, busily monitoring her vital signs as well as those of her baby.

She lay facing the dark window, her back to him. From his vantage point, if he hadn't known better, he would never have suspected she was pregnant. Her shoulders and hips appeared slim beneath the bedcovers, her waist a shallow dip between the two.

He thought for a moment that she was asleep, then heard a low groan and watched as her fingers curled around the edge of the mattress. He waited until they slowly relaxed, then said quietly, "Addy?"

She glanced over her shoulder, and her eyes widened in surprise. Shifting awkwardly to her back, she stretched out a hand. "Mack."

Her voice was no more than a whisper, but the relief in it resonated through him and settled somewhere near his heart. He crossed to the bed and gripped her hand within his.

"I thought you were going home," she said.

"I was," he admitted, then shrugged. "Decided I didn't want to miss the birthday party."

She narrowed her eyes in suspicion. "Did Marjorie call you?"

Mindful of his promise, he avoided her question by asking one of his own. "How are you doing?"

"Okay, I guess." Tears filled her eyes and she shook her head. "I'm scared, Mack. More scared than I've ever been in my life."

He chafed her hand between his. "Everything's going to be all right." He tipped his head toward the row of equipment and teased her with a smile. "Hell, there's enough technology in this room to send a man to the moon and back. Getting a baby here safely ought to be a snap."

She glanced toward the machines and winced. "It does seem a bit much, doesn't it?"

"What I want to know is, do all patients get this kind of preferential treatment or is it reserved for hospital employees?"

She laughed softly. "Since I've never been a patient, I wouldn't know."

She opened her mouth to say something more, then slammed her eyes shut and emitted a low groan.

He tightened his fingers around hers. "Another pain?"

Her teeth gritted, she nodded.

He racked his brain, trying to remember the techniques he'd learned in the Lamaze classes he'd attended with his wife. "Look at me," he ordered.

She opened her eyes and fixed them on his.

"Breathe slowly," he instructed. "Work with the pain, not against it."

He kept his gaze on hers while she hauled in a deep breath, released it, drew in another. Unconsciously he matched his breathing to hers, while he waited for the pain to pass. After what seemed like hours, her grip on his hand slowly relaxed and she released a long shuddery breath.

"Better?" he asked.

She wet her lips, nodded. "They're coming faster now. Harder."

He gave her hand a reassuring squeeze. "You're doing just fine. A couple more like that one, and I'll bet that baby will be here in no time."

"I'm going to hold you to—"

Her eyes went wide, her body rigid.

Without thinking, he laid a hand on her stomach and felt the tautness beneath his palm and knew she was already having another contraction. "Relax," he soothed, and began stroking his palm over her stomach.

Eyes wild, she fought him, struggling to escape his hold on her, as well as the pain.

He clamped down hard on her hand, refusing to let go. "Look at me, Addy," he ordered sternly. "Focus. We can do this."

She shook her head wildly. "Maybe you can, but I can't. It hurts!"

"It won't last forever." He increased the pressure on her hand. "Come on, Addy. Look at me. Focus."

She opened her eyes and bared her teeth. "I hate

you," she snarled. "You're mean and hateful and I wish you'd get the hell out of here and leave me alone."

Mack ignored her, knowing it was the pain talking. His wife had hurled similar accusations at him—and worse—while giving birth.

"Hate me all you want," he told her, "but I'm staying. We're going to get through this. Together. Now breathe."

She tried to wrench her hand away, then jackknifed to a sitting position, her eyes wide, her fingers clamped around his hard enough to crush bone. "It's coming!" she screamed. "Oh, God, get the nurse. The baby's coming!"

Mack grabbed the remote control clipped to the bed rail and punched the call button. Within seconds the door opened and a nurse strode into the room. She took one look at Addy's face and shouldered Mack aside, taking his place beside the bed.

"How far apart are the contractions?" she asked, as she checked Addy's pulse.

Mack dragged a shaky hand down his face, more than happy to relinquish control to the nurse. "Less than a minute."

The door opened again and a doctor sauntered in. "How's my favorite patient?"

Mack burned him with a look. "How do you think?" he snapped impatiently. "She's hurting like hell and needs something for the pain."

"No!" Addy cried and fell back against the pillows, holding her hands protectively over her stomach. "No drugs. I'm doing this naturally."

The doctor looked at Mac and shrugged as if to say

"you heard the woman," then stepped to the end of the bed and lifted the sheet to visibly check her progress.

"The head's crowned," he reported, then dropped the sheet and strode to the sink, his steps quicker now, his expression all business. As he squirted disinfectant on his hands, he glanced Mack's way. "If you're the father, you'll need to scrub up. Otherwise—" he tipped his head toward the door "—the waiting room's at the end of the hall."

Addy lunged, managing to catch Mack's sleeve. He glanced back and saw the fear in her eyes, the pleading. He set his jaw, knowing there was no way in hell he could leave her to face this birth alone.

"Where do I scrub?"

Mack sat in the chair by the window, his long legs stretched out in front of him and his head tipped back against the cushion, staring at the ceiling. Though exhausted, he couldn't sleep. His mind was racing, his body charged with adrenaline…and all because of the tiny bit of humanity, swaddled in a blue blanket and sleeping peacefully in the bassinet across the room.

He dropped his chin to look in that direction, and his heart did a slow flip. A boy, he thought, and had to swallow back the emotion that filled his throat, weighing in at a fraction over five pounds but healthy as a horse and with a set of lungs to prove it. Though there had been concerns that the baby wouldn't be fully developed, he'd passed all the tests like a champ, and wouldn't have to spend any time in an incubator, as most preemies were required to do.

Unable to resist, he heaved himself from the chair and crossed to peer down at the baby. Bundled up snug in the blue blanket, only the infant's face was visible, revealing rosy cheeks and a nose no bigger than a button. Dark fuzz covered his head, but Mack knew from experience that he'd probably lose it and what grew back might be a different color entirely. His own son's hair had been coal-black at birth, but by the age of two, it was cotton white. He wondered what color it would've been if he'd lived?

Stifling a groan, he dropped his chin to his chest. He didn't want to think about his son. Not now. Remembering made him hurt, and Mack had hurt for too many years.

Taking a deep breath, he lifted his head and stared hard, until he succeeded in shoving back the memory and was able to bring the baby into focus again.

His smile wistful, he reached to smooth the back of his fingers over the baby's cheek, marveling at its softness, the miniature features.

"You're one lucky guy," he whispered to the sleeping infant. "You've got a helluva mother. Even when the pain was really bad, she wouldn't let them give her anything to ease it, for fear it would hurt you." He smoothed a knuckle across the baby's opposite cheek. "Trust me. That kind of love is a rare thing."

The baby scrunched up his face, as if preparing to cry.

"Whoa, now," Mack warned and quickly lifted the baby from the bassinet. "None of that. You don't want to wake up your mom, now, do you?"

Cradling the baby in his arms, he tiptoed back to the

chair and eased down. The infant yawned, rooted around a moment, then settled back to sleep, holding one hand curled in a fist against his cheek.

Mack stared at the infant, and his heart seemed to stop, then kicked into a pounding beat. The baby's coloring and features mimicked those of his son so closely, he could be Mack's child. Unable to tear his gaze away, he stared, his heart thundering against his rib cage, as he wondered if this baby was an answer to the problem that had been troubling him lately.

Though he considered it morbid to think about his own death, that's exactly what he'd been doing for the better part of a year. He supposed it was a sign that he was getting old, for him to be having such thoughts—although he didn't consider forty-two all that old. But death was a fact of life, the same as living, and he was aware, especially with an estate the size of his, that he should have a will in place, no matter what his age or state of health. Having one drawn one up was easy enough. All he had to do was call his lawyer. What kept him from making the call was his lack of an heir. Most men named their wives or kids as their beneficiaries, or a combination of the two. But Mack didn't have a wife or children...at least, none that were living.

He'd lost his wife and son in a senseless car wreck twelve years before and had never remarried. For the first couple of years following their deaths, he'd found it hard enough to breathe, much less think about marrying again. But even after the pain of losing them had dulled somewhat, he still hadn't been able to work up the enthusiasm to ask a woman out on a date.

When asked, he claimed it was because he'd never met one that caught his eye. But the truth was, he'd never looked. Losing his wife and son had changed him, stripping him of the desire to develop attachments with anyone, especially a woman. As a result, he'd reached the ripe old age of forty-two with no family, other than his half brother, to name in a will.

He scowled at the reminder of Ty. Hell, if he left his estate to his half brother, everything Mack and Mack's father before him had worked and struggled to build would be lost in less than a year's time. Ty had the business acumen of a jackass and the attention span of a two-year-old. He looked at everything in terms of what he could turn it for and the fun it would buy him when he did.

No, he wouldn't leave his estate to Ty.

Mack focused his gaze on the baby again, wondering if the child could be the answer to his problem. He could adopt him, he told himself. Raise the boy as his own, ingrain in him the morals and integrity that the child would never learn if left up to Ty.

Ty didn't care about the kid, Mack told himself. If he did, he'd be here right now, instead of playing an adult version of hide and seek. If he'd felt any sense of responsibility at all, Ty would've been the one holding Addy's hand while the baby was born, not Mack. And it would've been Ty, not Mack, who the doctor had passed the scissors to and allowed to cut the umbilical cord, signifying the baby's official entry into the world.

The way Mack looked at it, his willingness to adopt

the baby was the perfect solution to everyone's problems. The child would have a father, Ty would be off the hook, and Mack would have an heir.

There was only one problem…the baby's mother.

In spite of the bond Mack and Addy had forged during the last fourteen-plus hours, he doubted she would embrace the idea if he were to suggest him adopting her baby. In fact, she'd probably think he'd lost his mind.

"Mack?"

He jumped at the sound of Addy's voice and glanced up to find her peering at him curiously.

"Is something wrong?" she asked in concern.

Fearing she would somehow read his thoughts and know what he'd been thinking, he dropped his gaze and tucked the blanket more snugly at the baby's chin. "No. He looked like he was going to start fussing, and I thought if I held him awhile, it would give you the chance to sleep a little longer."

Her smile tender, she eased herself to a sitting position and held out her arms. "Here. Give him to me. I'll bet he's hungry."

Rising, Mack carried the baby to the bed and settled the infant in her arms.

As if sensing his nearness to his milk supply, the baby twisted his head toward her breast, his mouth open like a baby's birds.

Addy placed a finger against the infant's lips and laughed when he began to suck. "See?" she said, and began to rearrange her nightgown. "He is hungry."

She stopped and glanced up at Mack, her cheeks

stained a deep rose, as if she'd just realized the intimacy of what she was preparing to do.

He immediately took a step back. "I'll wait outside," he said, and turned for the door.

"No! Wait."

He glanced over his shoulder, surprised by the panic in her voice.

Dropping her gaze, she fluttered a hand. "Just turn your back until I get him situated."

Mack did as instructed and waited until he heard her signal of "ready" before turning around. Finding her and the baby modestly covered by the blue blanket, he reached behind him to drag his chair closer to the bed.

"Its amazing how a baby instinctively knows how to nurse," he said softly, awed by the sight.

Her gaze on the infant, she smiled. "Yes, it is."

Moments passed in silence, both absorbed by the baby's movements.

"Mack?"

His attention focused on the nursing infant, he mumbled a distracted, "Yeah?"

"I'm sorry."

He angled his head to peer at her in puzzlement. "For what?"

"For all the mean things I said to you while I was in labor."

He waved away the apology. "I knew you didn't mean any of that stuff. That was the pain talking."

"Just the same, I'm sorry. I don't know what I would've done without you."

He choked out a laugh. "Heck, I had the easy part. You were the one who was doing all the work."

She looked down at the baby and smiled. "And look what I got for my trouble. A beautiful, healthy baby. I couldn't ask for anything more."

"He's a keeper, all right."

The door opened and Marjorie sailed in, trailing a balloon bouquet in her wake. Without so much as a how-do-you-do to Mack or Addy, she headed straight for the bed, her gaze on the baby.

"Oh, let me see that little tiger," she said eagerly, as she tethered the streamers of the balloon bouquet at the head of the bed.

Addy deftly separated the baby from her breast, rearranged her nightgown, then folded back the blanket, for Marjorie to see. "Isn't he beautiful?"

"Gorgeous," Marjorie agreed, then tipped her face up to Addy's. "Have you named him yet?"

Addy shook her head. "No. I had a girl's name picked out, but I hadn't settled on one for a boy."

"I thought you were going to use your father's name?" Marjorie said.

"Only his first name." She shrugged. "I haven't been able to come up with anything that sounds right with Antonio."

Marjorie pursed her lips thoughtfully, then swung her gaze to Mack. "What's your full name?"

Caught off-guard, Mack blinked, then stammered, "Uh, Jonathan Michael McGruder."

"What about Antonio Michael Rocci?" Marjorie suggested to Addy.

Frowning, Addy shook her head. "I want to use Antonio as his middle name."

"Then name him Jonathan Antonio Rocci. You could call him Johnny."

"Jonathan Antonio Rocci," Addy repeated, as if testing the sound of the name, then nodded. "It's a mouthful, but I like it." She glanced at Mack, her expression hopeful. "Would you mind if I gave my baby your name?"

Mind? Mack thought. Hell, he was hoping he could persuade her to give the baby his last name, as well. "I'd be honored."

The pager in Marjorie's pocket beeped and she pulled it out to check the display. "Those imbeciles," she muttered crossly. "You'd think they could run the ER for ten minutes without me." She slid the pager back into her pocket and offered Addy an apologetic smile. "Sorry, hon, but I've got to scoot. I'll try to come back later, when I'm on my dinner break."

"Call first," Addy warned. "I'm hoping I can persuade Dr. Wharton to release me."

Marjorie wagged a finger at her nose. "You listen to me, young lady. You've just had a baby. You have no business going home to an empty house. You stay right here where the nursing staff can take care of you and the baby."

Addy jutted her chin. "I can take care of myself."

"But—"

"No, Marjorie," she said, cutting her friend off. "I'm going home."

With a huff of disgust, Marjorie turned to leave. "*You* try talking some sense into that thick head of hers," she said to Mack. "She won't listen to me."

Mack had remained quiet during the exchange, absorbing the conversation and considering how he could use the situation to his own advantage. He knew the idea to adopt the baby was a crazy one and liable to send Addy into an apoplectic fit. But the more he thought about it, the more he was convinced it was the best solution to all their problems, both his and Addy's.

Now he just had to convince her of that.

He waited until the door closed behind Marjorie, then said quietly, "She's right, you know. It doesn't make sense for you to go home, when you have all the help you need right here."

Her lips pursed in annoyance, Addy bundled the sleeping baby back up into the blanket. "Marjorie's a buttinsky. She's forever sticking her nose in other people's business."

When he saw that she intended to carry the baby back to his bassinet, Mack stood. "Here. I'll take him." He took the baby from her and crossed to the bassinet. "She's only thinking of what's best for you," he said, refocusing the conversation on Marjorie's suggestion.

Addy folded her arms stubbornly across her chest. "I can take care of myself."

Mack glanced over his shoulder. "Like you were last night when I found you?"

She opened her mouth, then closed it, the blood slowly draining from her face.

Mack knew what he'd said was mean, even cruel, but he felt it was necessary, if he was going to convince Addy that she needed his help.

He crossed to sit beside the bed again. "Once you're able to return to work, what happens if you get sick? Who'll look after the baby then?"

She nervously wet her lips. "I...I'll manage."

"How, Addy?" he persisted. "Your mother certainly won't come to your rescue. I've talked to her. In fact, her last words to me were, 'she's the one who got herself into this mess, and she'll have to see it to its end.'"

She dropped her gaze, but not before he saw the tears that brimmed in her eyes.

He reached out a hand and laid it on her arm. "I'm not trying to hurt you, Addy," he said quietly. "I'm only trying to make you see that you can't do this alone."

She dragged a hand beneath her nose. "Like I have a choice."

It was the opening Mack had hoped for, needed. "I'd be willing to help you."

She snapped her gaze to his. "*You?* Why would you want to help me? You don't even know me."

He kept his gaze fixed on hers. "I know more than you might think."

When her forehead pleated in confusion, he decided it was time to tell all. "I know that the father of your baby isn't going to be around to take care of you and the baby."

Her jaw dropped, then closed with an angry click of teeth. "You don't know any such thing."

"Yes, I do," he replied calmly. "If his past actions are any indication, you'll never hear from Ty Bodean again."

Her eyes shot wide. "You…you know Ty?"

"He's my half brother."

"He's your…" She gulped, swallowed. "You mean, you knew about me and the baby, before…"

"Yes. The letters you sent to Ty in care of the postmaster of Lampasas were delivered to my house."

If possible, her eyes widened even more. "You *read* them?"

"Yes," he admitted. "Though not at first. It wasn't until the third letter arrived that I decided I should open them, so I could find out what kind of trouble Ty had gotten himself into." He shook his head sadly. "You aren't the first person whose attempts to track Ty down have led to me. I had to read your letters so I'd know what I was dealing with."

She dropped her face to her hands. "Oh, my God," she moaned.

Mack laid a hand on her arm. "I'm not telling you this to embarrass you."

She snapped her head up to glare at him. "Then why are you? I may be slow, but I'm not stupid. I'd figured out that Ty was never coming back." She snatched her arm from beneath his hand. "You didn't need to drive all the way to Dallas to tell me *that*."

Sighing, Mack slowly drew his hand back to rest it on his thigh. "That's not why I went to your house. I went there to offer you money."

Steam all but came out of her ears. "Well, you can tell Ty Bodean to keep his damn money. I don't want it."

"The money's not Ty's. It's mine."

"Well, I don't want your money, either," she snapped. She pointed a stiff finger at the door. "Get out. And don't bother coming back. I never want to see you again. Ever."

Three

Mack figured he'd pretty much blown his chances of convincing Addy to allow him to adopt her baby…but that didn't mean he was ready to throw in the towel. It wasn't in his nature to concede defeat, not without first putting up a damn good fight.

And as far as Mack was concerned, the battle had only just begun.

In retrospect, he could see his mistakes…and he'd made some doozies. The first was blindsiding Addy with the news that he was Ty's half brother. Considering how she must feel toward Ty after he'd abandoned her, Mack should have suspected that she would want nothing to do with anyone even remotely related to his half brother.

His second mistake was in telling her he'd gone to her home to offer her money. In the less than twenty-four hours he'd known Addy, he had seen evidence of a strong pride, as well as a pretty wide stubborn streak. Offering a payoff to a woman like her would be an insult, a slap on the face. She wouldn't care about money or the lack thereof. A woman like her was ruled by her heart. She'd willingly sacrifice anything for those she loved…and she'd accept nothing as a replacement for it, not even money. How Mack knew that about her, he wasn't sure, but he'd bet his ranch that he'd pegged her right.

Since he was certain he'd destroyed whatever level of trust he'd managed to establish with her over the past twenty-four hours, he figured he would need some help winning it back, and that was going to require some fancy two-stepping. But Mack was prepared to wear out the soles of his boots, if that's what it took.

After checking into a hotel near the hospital, he made several phone calls, the first to his lawyer. He explained the situation and told his lawyer what he needed from him. Then he placed calls to his pastor, his banker and lastly to his best friend, who also happened to be a highly respected and well-known pediatrician in Mack's hometown.

After obtaining their assurance that they would do all they could to assist him, he then called Addy's doctor, knowing he would need the support and backing of people she knew and respected. The last call he made was to Marjorie. He quickly outlined his plan to Addy's friend and was relieved when she promised to do everything within her power to convince Addy to go along with it.

Satisfied that he'd done all that he could to ensure a positive outcome for the meeting he had arranged for the next morning, Mack fell into bed, exhausted, not realizing until the moment his head hit the pillow that he hadn't slept in more than forty-eight hours.

Addy checked the room one last time to make sure that she hadn't forgotten anything. Since her stay at the hospital had been brief and so few people had known about it, there wasn't much for her to worry about. Thanks to Marjorie, who had dropped by Addy's house the evening before and picked up a few of her things, she'd had a clean set of clothes to put on that morning and an outfit for the baby to wear home. Other than herself, the baby and a small overnight bag, the only personal items in the room were the balloon bouquet Marjorie had given her, a vase of long-stemmed roses from the hospital staff and a huge basket filled with baby gifts from her co-workers in the ER. Now all she needed was for Dr. Wharton to make his morning rounds and sign her release, and she could call a taxi and go home.

She glanced at her wristwatch and frowned, wondering what was taking her doctor so long. Normally he was finished with his rounds by eight, and it was already ten after. Impatient to be on her way, she checked the baby to make sure he was still sleeping, then headed for the door to peek into the hall to see if her doctor was still on the floor.

Before she reached it, the door opened and Dr. Wharton stepped inside.

Her smile sheepish, she lifted her hands, then dropped them to her sides. "I was just on my way to look for you. I was afraid you'd forgotten about me."

He slung an arm around her shoulders and walked with her toward the bassinet. "Forget about my favorite patient?" he teased. "No way." He dropped his arm from around her and stooped to peer down at the baby. "And how's our little man doing this morning?" he asked.

"Perfect. He only woke me up once last night for a feeding."

He nodded his approval. "Then your milk must be satisfying him."

"Seems like."

The door opened behind her, and Addy glanced over her shoulder. Her eyes shot wide open, when she saw it was Mack, then narrowed dangerously.

"What are you doing here?" she said from between clenched teeth.

Ignoring her, he glanced toward Dr. Wharton and nodded. "Tom," he said, by way of greeting. "I appreciate you arranging your schedule so that you could meet with us this morning."

Addy was so stunned by Mack's casual usage of her doctor's first name that it took her a moment to absorb what else he'd said.

"What meeting?" she demanded to know.

"The one I arranged," Mack replied.

The door opened again and Marjorie came in.

Addy turned to glare at Mack. "Did you ask *her* to attend this meeting, too?"

"Yes. I thought you'd want her input."

"Input on what?" Addy asked in growing frustration.

"On how best to resolve your problems."

"*You* are my only problem," she said furiously.

"Now, Addy," Marjorie scolded gently. "At least hear what Mack has to say."

Before Addy could tell Marjorie to mind her own business, Dr. Wharton spoke up. "Marjorie's right, Addy. You need to listen to Mack's suggestion."

Addy folded her arms across her chest and burned Mack with a look. "All right. You've got exactly two minutes and not a second more."

"I want you to marry me," he said simply.

"What?" she cried. "Are you crazy?"

"No, I assure you I'm perfectly sane. I'm a wealthy man, Addy. I can provide a lifestyle for you and the baby that you could never accomplish alone."

When she opened her mouth to tell him what he could with his lifestyle, as well as his proposal, he held up a hand.

"Please, hear me out. What I'm suggesting is not a traditional marriage. I would make no demands on you, sexual or emotional. My offer of marriage is simply a way to provide for you and give your baby a name. I'm prepared to legally adopt your child and raise him as my own son. My home is large enough to provide you with whatever privacy you deem necessary, plus it's staffed with a housekeeper and cook who will see to yours and the baby's needs.

"If at some time in the future," he went on, "you should find our arrangement confining or you feel threatened in any way, then I will grant you an annulment but will continue to provide financial support for the child."

"Why would you want to support him, if we're no longer living with you?"

His gaze remained steady on hers, his expression maddeningly calm in spite of her accusatory tone.

"For the same reason I'm offering you marriage," he said simply. "To ensure that he is always provided for. I take care of what's mine."

He held up a finger when she would have interrupted him. "When I adopt your son, I'll be assuming not only the legal and financial obligations associated with him but the moral ones, as well. Because of that commitment, I would place one stipulation on granting you an annulment, should you request one. I want the same rights awarded any father at the time of a divorce. Specifically, an equitable visitation schedule and the right to remain an active participant in his life. By remaining involved, I can be sure that he is instilled with the virtues necessary for him to develop into a man of honor and integrity."

Addy stared, part of her awed by what appeared to be his sincere concern for her son, and the other part unable to believe he would actually expect her to agree to such an outlandish arrangement.

"Do you have any idea what you're asking of me?" she said to him, then looked at Dr. Wharton and

Marjorie. "Do *you*?" she challenged. "I hardly know this man! Yes," she conceded, before either could remind her of the fact, "he probably saved my life and that of my baby, but prior to his coming to my rescue, I'd never seen him before! And you expect me to *marry* him?" she asked incredulously. "Are y'all crazy?"

"Mack has proven he's trustworthy," Marjorie argued. "He didn't have to follow the ambulance to the hospital, but he did. And he didn't have to turn around and drive back to Dallas when I called and told him that you'd gone into labor again. And, yes," she admitted, with a jut of her chin, when Addy narrowed her eyes at her, "I called him. So sue me."

"And he stayed with you throughout the delivery," Dr. Wharton interjected, taking over where Marjorie had left off. He dipped his chin and gave Addy a pointed look. "Which was at your request, as I recall."

She opened her hands. "I was delirious. Out of my mind with pain. Why else would I beg a complete stranger, and a man at that, to stay with me during the birth of my baby?"

"I can understand why you might be hesitant to accept my proposal," Mack said patiently.

"Hesitant?" she repeated, her voice rising as she whirled to face him. "How about violently opposed!"

Ignoring her, he continued. "In order to satisfy whatever concerns you might have, I've taken it upon myself to provide you with suitable references." He crossed to the door and opened it. "Gentlemen," he said, and spread an arm in invitation. "Would you please join us?"

Addy stared, wide-eyed, as four men filed into the room. The first to enter approached her, his hand held out in greeting.

"Leonard Boyles, Attorney-at-Law," he said by way of introduction. "I handle all Mack's legal needs and have for years. I can assure you that he has never been accused of any crime or sued in a court of law. His record, as well as his reputation, are both without blemish."

Speechless, Addy could only stare.

As soon as the lawyer moved aside, a second man— a clergyman judging by his white collar—stepped forward and gathered her hand between his.

"Pastor Nolan, my child," he said in a voice that invited trust. "I've served as Mack's spiritual advisor since he was a young boy and can honestly say that I've never known a finer man or one with a more generous heart. If you agree to marry him, it will be my honor to perform the ceremony."

Before Addy could think of a reply, a third man moved to stand before her.

"Jack Phelps," he said, and gave her a hand a brisk, no-nonsense shake. "President of Commerce Bank and Trust. Mack, as his father was before him, is a major stockholder in CB&T. As the bank's president, I can attest to Mack's financial soundness, and offer you my assurance that he's a well-respected leader in our community."

Numb, Addy could only nod.

The next man to step forward was large, both in girth and height, but the warmth and friendliness in his eyes thwarted any fear his size might've spawned.

"So you're Addy," he said, gripping her hand between bear-size paws. "Officially, I'm Dr. William Johnson," he said solemnly, then grinned. "But most folks just call me Dr. Bill." He glanced toward the bassinet, then shifted his gaze back to hers, his expression hopeful. "Mind if I hold the baby? I promise I won't wake him. I've had plenty of experience with little ones."

She lifted a hand, then dropped it helplessly to her side. "Why not?"

She watched as he lifted the baby from the bassinet and brought it to cradle against his chest.

"And aren't you just the cutest thing," he murmured to the baby, then looked up at her and smiled. "I know you must be proud."

She pressed a hand against her lips to stem an unexpected rush of tears. "Y-yes, I am," she managed to get out.

Clucking his tongue, he shifted the baby to one arm and moved to slip the other around her shoulder. "Now, now," he soothed, as he hugged her against his side. "It's okay to cry. Mood swings are to be expected in new mothers."

Addy had to fight the urge to turn her face against his chest and sob. "I know," she said, dabbing at her eyes. "I'm a nurse. I did a rotation in Labor and Delivery during my clinicals, so I know all about the baby blues."

He drew back to look at her in surprise. "You're a nurse? Then I guess I don't need to tell you how important it is for a new mother to take it easy the first couple of weeks, following childbirth. Takes time for a woman to heal properly and regain her strength. Did I mention that I'm a pediatrician?" he asked, then looked down at the baby before she could respond, and smiled broadly. "This little guy and I are going to get along just fine. After you get settled in at Mack's, bring him over to my office and we'll give him a complete checkup."

"But I'm—"

He hugged her again, nearly squeezing the breath out of her with his enthusiasm. "You're gonna just love living in Lampasas. I just know you are."

Addy twisted from his arms and balled her hands into fists at her sides. "Would someone please listen to me," she cried. "I'm *not* marrying Mack. Okay? *I'm not marrying Mack!*"

Marjorie rushed forward and caught her hand. "Oh, Addy," she whispered urgently. "Think what he's offering you. A worry-free life. You wouldn't have to work. You could stay at home with your baby, be the mother you've always wanted to be. And he's willing to adopt your son, give him his name. If you marry Mack, your baby will never be subjected to the embarrassment and humiliation you experienced growing up. He'll have a *name.* A father. People won't be able to whisper behind his back and call him ugly names like they did you."

Addy clamped her hand over her ears, sure that she could hear the jeers of the children who had taunted her on the playground, the whispered comments from adults. She didn't want her son to suffer as she had. Didn't want the same questions posed to him that were asked of her. *Where's your father? Who's your father? How come your mother's name isn't the same as yours?*

"Think, Addy," Marjorie begged her. "It's not as if you have to stay married to him. He's giving you an out, the offer of an annulment. What have you got to lose?"

Addy turned away, clamping her hands tighter over her ears. "Please," she begged. "Go. All of you. I need to think."

She heard the door open behind her and the shuffle of feet as the crowd of people in her room filed out. She felt a nudge on her shoulder, and glanced up to find Dr. Bill standing there.

He passed the baby to her, then braced a hand on her shoulder. "Mack's a good man," he said quietly. "Keep that in mind while you're doing your thinking."

He gave her shoulder a squeeze, then turned and left the room.

Blinking back tears, Addy hugged the baby to her breasts. "Oh, Johnny," she whispered tearfully. "What are we going to do?"

Holding the baby in her arms, Addy opened the door of her hospital room to find the group she'd ousted earlier standing in the hall. The lawyer, the banker, the preacher, Marjorie…and Mack. They were all there, except for Dr. Wharton, who she assumed had to leave because patients waited for him at his office.

Lined up as they were, those who remained presented a formidable wall of resistance.

She tipped up her chin, unwilling to show any sign of weakness. "You may come in," she informed them, then turned and led the way back into her room.

She waited until the door closed behind Mack, then directly addressed the lawyer. "If I agree to this, I want everything in writing, including Mack's promise of an annulment."

"Consider it done," he replied.

"And I want your assurance," she continued, "that my legal interests will be protected, as well as those of my son."

He held up a hand in a solemn pledge. "You have my word."

Satisfied, she shifted her gaze, meeting the eyes of each person in turn.

"You all heard what Mack said earlier, and I expect each and every one of you to serve as witnesses to the document the lawyer prepares. And be forewarned," she added sternly, "that I intend to hold each of you personally responsible for my welfare and that of my son, should Mack fail to honor the promises he's made to me. Understood?"

Each person nodded their agreement.

She drew in a deep breath and turned to face Mack. "I assume you want this marriage to take place as soon as possible."

"Now will do."

"Now?" she repeated. "But…won't we need a license?"

He nodded toward his lawyer, who was already drawing a document from the inside pocket of his jacket. "Lenny has taken care of that for us."

A bubble of panic rose in Addy's throat. She'd thought

she'd have more time to adjust, to plan…to come to her senses. "Blood tests," she said in a rush. "The state requires blood tests, before they'll issue a license."

Marjorie lifted a meek hand. "Um. That's been taken care of."

"How?" Addy asked incredulously. "I didn't give any blood."

"Dr. Wharton told Kenny, the phlebotomist, to use some of what he drew the night you were admitted to Emergency."

With nothing left to offer to delay the inevitable, Addy dropped her shoulders in defeat and turned to Pastor Nolan. "Looks like it your turn, Preacher. I suppose it would be foolish to ask if you have your Bible with you?"

He drew a small leather-bound book from his pocket and held it up for her to see. "I'm never without it."

Though she tried her best to hide it, Addy was totally blown away by Mack's home. The driveway he had turned onto was lined with massive oaks, their limbs twining overhead to create the canopy of shade they drove through. The house at the end of the drive reminded her of pictures she'd seen in magazines of Tuscan homes. Built from a combination of stucco and stone, angled wings jutted from either side of the central structure to form what could only be described as an exploding U. Beyond it, rolling hills covered with cedar, cactus and rock, served as a dramatic backdrop for his home.

Mack parked his car on the circle drive in front, then

climbed out and opened the rear door to remove the baby from the car seat. Her knees quaking, Addy followed Mack up the flagstone walkway to the front door.

Just as Mack reached to open it, the door flew back and two women rushed into the opening, their shoulders bumping, as they both tried to pass through at the same time.

Mack held up a hand. "Slow down, ladies. You'll both get a chance to hold him."

He reached back to catch Addy's hand and drew her to stand beside him. "Addy, I'd like you to meet, Zadie, my cook. She has an apartment at the rear of the house and pretty much rules the roost. Cross her and she'll come after you with a wooden spoon."

Shaking her head, the larger of the two women stepped forward. "Don't believe a word the man says," she warned Addy. "The only person I've ever chased with a wooden spoon was him, and that was because he cut into the pie I'd made for his supper." Smiling, she bobbed her chin in greeting. "Pleased to meet you, Ms. Addy."

"And this is Mary," Mack said, with a nod toward the second woman. "She's here from eight to five, six days a week, chasing the dust balls around the house."

Small in stature but fiery, Mary planted her hands on her hips. "If you can find a dust ball in this house, Mr. Mack, I'll eat it." With a sniff, she turned her gaze to Addy and smiled. "Welcome home, Ms. Addy. If you need anything, anything at all, you just come to me and I'll take care of it for you."

Mary's gaze shifted to the baby and she rubbed her

hands together in excitement, as if anxious to steal him away from Mack.

"Uh-uh," Zadie warned and stepped in front of her blocking her way. "Me first. You've got babies at home to hold. I ain't got any."

Her smile tender, Zadie eased the baby from Mack's arms into her own. "Ain't he just the prettiest thing," she said softly, then looked up at Mack in surprise. "Why, Mr. Mack, he looks just like those baby pictures of you that used to hang in your mama's front room."

"He's got Mack's nose," Mary said, peering down at the baby, then glanced at Addy. "What's his name?"

Shocked that the women thought her son looked like Mack, it took Addy a moment to find her voice. "Jonathan Antonio Roc—uh, I mean McGruder."

"Mighty big name for such a little tyke," Zadie said, chuckling. "What's you gonna call him?"

"Johnny," Addy replied.

"Johnny, huh?" Zadie studied him a moment, then turned for the house. "Well, come on, Johnny Mack. Let's get you inside and out of this heat."

Addy blinked in surprise. Johnny Mack?

Mary darted after Zadie. "You give Johnny Mack to me. You've had him long enough."

Addy turned to peer at Mack in disbelief. "Did you hear them? They called him Johnny Mack."

With a shrug, Mack turned for the car to retrieve her luggage. "Lots of people around here have double names."

She charged after him. "But I clearly told them his

name is Jonathan Antonio. Why would they stick Mack on the end? Why not Tony?"

Bent over the trunk, he dragged a suitcase out and set it on the drive. "I suppose because he looks like me." He straightened to face her. "Which shouldn't surprise you, since Ty and I have the same mother. We may not look like twins, but we both inherited our mother's nose and the shape of her mouth."

Addy gulped. Having had the resemblance pointed out to her, she could see it now.

Mack picked up the suitcase and turned for the house. "If you want, I'll tell Zadie and Mary to drop the Mack and just call him Johnny."

"No," Addy said slowly, deciding not to chance upsetting the women.

And what did it matter, anyway? she asked herself, as she followed Mack to the house. It was just a nickname.

Addy knew exactly what Dorothy must have felt like when she awakened to find herself in Oz. She definitely wasn't in Kansas anymore.

The suite of rooms Mary had left her to explore were larger than most people's homes. Besides the tastefully furnished bedroom, there was a private bath, with a garden-size tub and mile-long, marble-topped vanity. A sitting room connected her bedroom to Mack's and had been converted to a nursery prior to their arrival, complete with a crib, changing table and rocker.

She wondered how Mack had managed to have the room transformed so quickly, then shook her head at the absurdity of the question. As he'd already proven to her, he obviously had the resources and connections to accomplish anything he darn well pleased.

With a sigh of resignation, she slipped into the nursery to make sure the baby was sleeping peacefully, then stepped through the French doors that opened from her bedroom onto a private patio. Surrounded by a stone wall, the area was subtly lit by copper landscape lights and was lush with colorful plants and tall, lacy ferns. In the far corner, a waterfall tumbled over stacked rocks and spilled into a small pond, where koi swam lazily beneath lily pads. Finding the sound of tumbling water as soothing to the ear as the garden setting was to the eye, Addy sank onto a lounge chair and allowed the tension to seep from her body.

It had been an exhausting day, both mentally and physically. First there was the stressful confrontation at the hospital with the friends and business associates Mack had rounded up to plead his case, followed by the brief and impersonal marriage ceremony. Then the trip to her house and the almost-manic grabbing and packing of the few possessions she had chosen to bring with her. Mack had offered to hire a moving service to pack everything up and deliver it to his home in Lampasas, but Addy had refused. She wasn't at all sure that the arrangement she'd made with him was going to work, and she wanted her home intact and waiting for her in the event it didn't.

And then there had been the long drive from Dallas to Lampasas. Most of it had been made in silence, as

Addy was still too shell-shocked from the morning's events to make any attempt at conversation. What faculties she had remaining were stripped from her completely when she got her first glimpse of his home. In spite of his assurance that morning that his home was large and more than adequate to provide her whatever privacy she deemed necessary, it had in no way prepared her for the palatial mansion that had greeted her.

But her shock over his home's size and his obvious wealth was nothing compared to what she'd experienced when Zadie had called her son Johnny Mack. She supposed Mack's explanation made sense, but she still couldn't believe she hadn't noticed the facial features that Mack and Ty shared before Mack had pointed them out to her.

The thought of Ty put the tension right back in her shoulders. Though Mack had told her that she needn't worry about Ty, she couldn't shake free from the thought that he might come back to haunt her in some way.

For God's sake, she thought, her worry returning with a vengeance. The two men were brothers! What would keep Ty from unexpectedly dropping by for a visit? The very thought of seeing him made her shudder in revulsion. She *never* wanted to lay eyes on Ty Bodean again. She might have once thought herself in love with him, but that was before she'd discovered that he was a liar and a thief.

"I hope you've found your accommodations adequate."

She jumped at the sound of Mack's voice, then gulped and rose slowly to face him, twisting her hands at her waist. "This isn't going to work."

He peered at her in concern. "Is there a problem with your room? If so, there are several others to choose from."

She turned away to pace. "There's nothing wrong with the room. It's beautiful."

"Then what's the problem?"

She whirled to face him. "Have you forgotten that the father of my child is your brother?"

"Half brother," he corrected, then opened his hands. "What difference does that make?"

"What if he comes here? He could cause trouble. Even try to take the baby away from me."

He took her by the arm and guided her back to her chair. "Ty can't take the baby. Lenny is already preparing the adoption papers. Once they're filed, Johnny will be legally mine."

"But he could contest the adoption, couldn't he? Demand a blood test to prove that he's the natural father?"

With a sigh he released her arm and sank down onto the chair next to her. "I suppose he could, but why would he? He knew you were pregnant when he left you. Why would he want to claim the child, when your pregnancy was why he ran away in the first place?" He covered her hand with his. "But you're worrying about nothing, Addy. Ty won't come to Lampasas, much less to my house."

"You don't know that."

"Oh, but I do," he told her, and withdrew his hand. "Ty would do almost anything to avoid seeing me."

Frowning, she dragged the back of her hand across her stomach to ease the tingle his touch had left there. "You never talk to each other?"

"Rarely. And when we do, it's by phone, never in person."

He leaned back and stretched his legs out, his expression confident. "But even if he did come here, he'd never get past the front gate. He doesn't know the security code, and no one who works for me would let him in without asking my permission first." He angled his head to meet her gaze. "You're safe here, Addy. Both you and the baby. I'd never allow harm to come to either one of you."

She searched his face, wanting to believe him but afraid to let down her guard. Ty had looked her square in the eye and told her lie, after lie, after lie. Mack could be lying to her, too. Not only about his ability to protect her from Ty, but about his reasons for marrying her, as well. For all she knew, he could be planning to take advantage of her the same as Ty had.

But what could he possibly want from her? she asked herself honestly. Mack had no reason to steal from her, as Ty had. According to his banker, he was a wealthy man. And there was no way he'd want a physical relationship with her. For God's sake, she'd just had a baby! He'd seen her at her absolute worst, had even stood by her side while she'd given birth. If that wasn't a turn-off, she didn't know what was.

She supposed it was possible that he was telling the truth. The men he'd brought to the hospital to vouch for him had described him as a wealthy and generous man, and had sworn that he wasn't crazy, as she had accused him of being. And he seemed to genuinely care about her son.

"All right," she said reluctantly, then held up a finger in warning. "But if Ty should come here, I don't want him anywhere near me or my son. If you allow that to happen, I'll leave. Understood?"

"Fair enough." Flattening his hands against his thighs, he pushed to his feet with a sigh. "I have some paperwork I need to take care of in my office before I turn in. If you want, you can watch TV in the den."

She shook her head. "No. I think I'll go on to bed. It's been a long day."

He dropped a hand on her shoulder as he passed her and gave it a squeeze. "Good night, Addy."

Eyes wide, she murmured, "'Night," then listened to the sound of his footsteps, followed by the soft click of the door as it closed behind him. When she was sure she was alone, she tugged her shirt down over her shoulder and examined her skin, expecting to find a rash there, or at the very least a red mark. When she found neither, frowning, she dragged her shirt back into place, wondering what it was that made her skin tingle every time he touched her.

Four

Addy moaned, trying to block the voice that threatened her sleep.

"Addy," it persisted. "Wake up."

She slowly forced her eyes open and nearly jumped out of her skin when she found a man's shadowed face inches from her own. Recognizing it as Mack's, she went limp with relief. "You nearly scared the life out of me."

"Sorry, but the baby's hungry."

Instantly awake, she dragged herself up to a sitting position and held out her arms. "God, I'm sorry," she said guiltily. "I never heard him make so much as a peep."

He shifted the baby into her arms. "He didn't wake me. I heard him stirring when I got up to get a drink of water. Figured I'd rock him for a while, so you could sleep a little longer."

Grateful for the darkness, she quickly adjusted her nightgown so that the baby could nurse. "I appreciate the thought, but you didn't have to do that. I'm getting plenty of rest."

"I didn't mind."

Instead of leaving as she'd thought he would, he sank down on the edge of the bed and tucked the blanket around a bare foot the baby had managed to kick free. "In fact, I enjoyed rocking him," he added. "Brought back a few memories."

She heard the wistfulness in his voice and wondered about it. "Do you have children?"

"A son. He died when he was six."

"Oh, Mack," she said, her heart breaking for him at his loss. "I'm so sorry."

He lifted a shoulder. "It happened over twelve years ago. Time has a way of lessening the pain."

"Still…" She glanced down at her son, unable to imagine what it would do to her to lose him. As she considered that, it occurred to her that if Mack had a son, he probably had a wife, too.

"You're divorced?" she asked hesitantly.

"Widowed. My wife and son died together. A car wreck," he explained, saving her from asking.

She stared at his shadowed face, unable to fathom the magnitude of that kind of loss. "That must have been very hard for you."

"You have no idea."

Because she didn't, she turned her gaze to her son and said nothing.

They sat in silence while the baby nursed, the soft suckling noises the infant made the only sound in the room.

"Better change sides," Mack warned. "You don't want him to fill his tummy before he nurses your other breast."

"Right," she murmured, and placed a finger between her breast and the infant's mouth to separate him from her nipple. She started to shift him to her shoulder to burp, but on impulse, offered him to Mack. "Do you want to burp him?"

He sat up. "Yeah, I would."

With an ease that might've surprised her if she hadn't just learned that he'd once had a son, he placed the baby over his shoulder and began lightly patting his back. It wasn't until that moment that she realized Mack was wearing only a pair of jeans. Though she tried not to stare, she couldn't help but notice the dark hair that swirled around his nipples before plunging in a shadowed line down his abdomen to disappear behind the waist of his jeans, the bulge of muscles in his arms, as he held the baby.

The baby's loud burp made her start.

Chuckling, Mack said, "Good one," and passed the infant to Addy.

Amused, she guided the baby to her opposite breast. Though the darkness offered its own form of cover, she found it odd that she didn't feel more self-conscious about nursing in front of Mack. She supposed his presence during the birth had stripped her of whatever shyness she would ordinarily have experienced.

She lifted her head and looked at him curiously. "Do you consider this weird?"

His forehead pleated in confusion. "What?"

"This," she said, and lifted her arms slightly to indicate the baby. "Me nursing in front of you."

He pressed a palm against the mattress, as if about to rise. "If you want me to go—"

She laid a hand on his arm. "No. I was just thinking how odd it is to be doing this in front of a complete stranger."

"I'm hardly a stranger," he said wryly, as he settled back on the side of the bed. "I'm your husband."

Hearing him refer to himself as such was a little unsettling. "That may be true," she conceded, "but we've only known each other…what? Two days?"

He glanced at his wrist watch. "Two and a half," he corrected.

She sputtered a laugh. "Right. And that half day makes all the difference in the world."

"I've known people longer than I have you and know less about them."

She raised a brow, intrigued. "Oh? And what do you know about me?"

"You're stubborn as a mule."

"Well, that's certainly flattering," she said dryly.

Biting back a smile, he stretched out across the bed at her feet and braced himself up on an elbow. "I wasn't finished."

"I'm not sure my ego can stand hearing any more."

"You're brave, independent, resourceful."

She nodded smugly. "Now you're talking."

"And you're really good at hiding your feelings."

She looked at him in dismay. "Are you kidding? How can you say that, after all the fuss I kicked up about marrying you."

"I'm talking about the emotions you don't let anyone see."

"Oh? And exactly what emotions have I been hiding?"

"The ones concerning your mother. Her inattentiveness hurts you."

Embarrassed that he knew that about her, she averted her gaze but remained silent.

"She doesn't deserve you. You're a much better daughter to her than she is a mother to you."

The compliment, though sounding sincere, irritated her. "You don't know that. You've never even met her."

"I've talked to her. That was enough."

She rolled her eyes. "I disagree, but go on. Tell me what else you *think* you know about me."

"You're disappointed in yourself for letting a man like Ty get you pregnant."

Her embarrassment morphed to anger in the blink of an eye. "You make it sound as if I *tried* to get pregnant. I insisted he use condoms. Obviously one of them was flawed."

He patted the air, as if to calm her. "I worded that poorly. Let me try again. You're disappointed in yourself for becoming intimate with Ty. To be honest, I'm a bit surprised myself. You don't seem at all his type."

Though he was right about her regrets concerning Ty, she wasn't about to admit to her gullibility. "So what type am I?"

"The type who wants the whole package. Love, marriage, family. The whole ball of wax."

She stared, wondering if she was truly that transparent or if Marjorie had done more blabbing than Addy was aware. "And how did you arrive at that conclusion?"

"First, your house. The flowers along the walkway. The baskets of ferns on the porch. The bird feeder hanging from the tree out front."

"And from *that* you deduced that I'm Suzy Home-maker?" She tipped her head back and laughed. "You are *so* wrong."

"Am I?" he challenged. "Then why did you have the baby?"

She sputtered a laugh. "There was a choice?"

"Other single women in your situation have chosen to have abortions, rather than be saddled with a baby."

"So I'm pro-life. Shoot me."

"More like pro-family," he argued. "You may not have intended to get pregnant, but you weren't about to destroy your chance of having a family, even if it was missing one important element. The father."

Irritated that he was so close to the truth, she lifted the baby to her shoulder. "Okay, Freud. That's enough psychoanalysis for one night. I want to go to sleep."

He stood and held out his arms. "I'll put him to bed."

She resisted a moment, tempted to tell him that she was more than capable of putting her own child to bed, then decided why argue, when he had to pass through the nursery on the way to his room, anyway.

After handing over Johnny, she slid down and pulled the covers to her chin. "Don't forget to cover him up," she called to him.

"I know the drill."

In spite of her irritation with him, a smile tugged at the corners of her mouth. She could get used to this, she thought, as she nestled her cheek against the pillow.

It was kind of nice having someone wait on her for a change…even if the someone who was doing the waiting was a bossy know-it-all.

From the rocking chair, Addy watched Mary bustle from the bedroom to the nursery and back, putting away the baby's things. After over a week in Mack's house, she still couldn't get used to people waiting on her.

"Mary, really," she scolded gently. "You don't need to put those things away. It's enough that you're doing our laundry. Just leave the basket on the bed, and I'll put everything away later."

"It's no trouble," Mary insisted. Dipping into the basket again, she pulled out a sleeper from the pile of clothes she'd laundered and held it up to admire. "Oh, and isn't this just the sweetest thing," she said, and couldn't resist pressing the sleeper against her cheek. "Reminds of me when my kids were babies."

"How many children do you have?"

"Four."

"Four?" Addy repeated, then glanced down at the

baby placidly nursing at her breast and wondered how on earth a mother took care of that many children, when one seemed to her a full-time job. "How do you do it?"

Chuckling, Mary plucked out a blanket to fold. "Didn't you know? Mothers come equipped with an extra pair of hands."

Addy glanced down at her own and frowned. "I was cheated."

"How?"

Addy looked up to find Mack standing in the doorway…and had to blink twice to make sure it was him. Dressed in scuffed boots, faded jeans and with his hair mussed from the wind, he looked younger and much less imposing than the stone-faced man who, less than a week before, had promised to love and cherish her until death did them part.

She averted her gaze, still finding it hard to think of him as her husband.

"Mary says that mothers are given an extra set of hands," she explained. "I told her I was cheated, because I only have one."

He gestured toward the baby. "Little thing like that? One set is all you need." He started toward her. "Give him to me. You women have had him all morning. It's my turn."

Daddy's home! That wasn't at all what he'd said, but those were the words that shot into Addy's mind as he strode toward her, wiping his hands across the seat of his pants and wearing a grin that stretched from ear to ear.

Rising, she passed him the baby, then stepped aside, letting him have the rocker.

As Mack sat down, Johnny began to fuss, and Mack looked up at Addy in alarm. "Did I do something wrong?"

"Probably needs burping." She pulled the burp pad from her shoulder and draped it over Mack's. "He just finished nursing."

He shifted the baby up high on his chest and began to rub his back. "Come on little guy," he murmured, pressing a kiss to the top of the baby's head. "Give ol' Mack a big burp."

Johnny Mack complied almost instantly.

Laughing, Mary picked up the empty laundry basket. "Looks like you haven't lost your touch," she called to Mack, as she left the room.

Addy saw the shadow that passed over Mack's eyes and knew Mary's comment must have reminded him of his son. Hoping to distract him from what must be a sad memory, Addy sat down on the side of the bed opposite the rocker.

"Mary is determined to spoil me. She did Johnny's laundry this morning, then insisted on putting it all away."

Mack shifted the baby to cradle in his arms, but kept his gaze averted. "She's crazy about kids. Always has been."

Addy racked her mind for something else to say. "Has she worked for you a long time?"

"Fourteen years. Worked for my mother before that. I hired her on after Mom passed away."

"Did Zadie work for your mother, too?"

"Yes, but she went to work for a restaurant in town after my mother passed away. After my wife died, I realized I needed a cook, so I stole her away from the restaurant. She's been with me now about six years I guess."

Reminded of the delicious meals Zadie had prepared, she pressed a hand against her stomach. "I can understand why you'd want to steal her, but how on earth do you keep from getting fat? Much more of her cooking, and I'll have to revert to wearing maternity clothes again."

"Zadie says you eat like a bird."

Her jaw dropped. "You've seen how much I eat! We share every meal. I clean my plate."

"But refuse seconds."

She thought of the second helping of coconut cake Zadie had waved beneath her nose the night before, with its thick, creamy filling and the sprinkles of toasted coconut on the icing, and moaned pitifully. "The woman should be shot. How am I supposed to lose weight, when she keeps shoving those fabulous desserts in my face?"

"I'll tell her to cut out the sweets."

Fearing that she had just cut off her nose to spite her face, Addy said, "Uh, maybe you shouldn't say anything. I wouldn't want to take a chance on hurting Zadie's feelings."

He shot her a sideways glance. "Is it Zadie's feelings you're worried about or satisfying your sweet tooth?"

Pursing her lips, she snatched the burp pad from his shoulder and slapped his arm with it. "Jerk."

He ducked, chuckling. "That's what I thought."

He looked down at the baby and his smile slowly

faded. He caught a dribble of milky drool with his thumb and wiped it on the leg of his jeans. "Thanks," he said quietly.

She frowned at him in confusion. "For what?"

"For pulling me back." He angled his head to look at her. "Remembering hurts."

Addy sucked in a breath, stunned by the pain she saw in his blue eyes, the years of sorrow she saw stacked behind it. More than anything, she wanted to cup a hand at his cheek and soothe away the sadness, take away the hurt.

Before she could give in to the urge, she stood abruptly and held out her arms. "I better take him so you can get back to work. I'm sure you've got things to do."

He turned his shoulder to block her. "Nothing that can't wait. Go on and relax while you can." He glanced down at the baby and smiled. "Johnny Mack and I need us some man time."

Addy lay on a chaise lounge on her private patio, her eyes closed, the sun warm on her skin. A ring of condensation pooled around the tall glass of lemonade that stood within easy reach of her hand, while the magazine she'd been reading lay open over her stomach, marking her page. She felt relaxed, lazy even, and sinfully content.

To say she had landed in heaven wouldn't be much of an exaggeration, she thought with a sigh. Mack's home was lavish, the food five-star-restaurant quality, her every need met before she could voice it. And she never had to lift so much as a finger. Zadie cooked all the meals, while Mary took care of the cleaning and laundry. All Addy was allowed to do was care for the baby, and even that small task was lightened by the three other adults in the house, who were constantly looking for an excuse to steal Johnny away from her. New mothers need their rest, Mary would claim and disappear with the baby. Babies need constant stimulation, Zadie would say and whisk the baby off to the kitchen where a playpen had been set up by a wide set of French doors.

Then there was Mack. And of the three, he was the absolute worst. If Addy didn't know better, she'd swear he slept on the floor beside the crib at night. Before the baby could open his mouth to cry, Mack was in the nursery changing his diaper. He would rock him a while to make sure he was hungry and not just lonely, before delivering him to Addy. And he seldom left after bringing her the baby. He would usually stretch out across the bed at her feet and keep her company while the baby nursed.

She knew it was foolish, but she'd begun to look forward to that time with Mack. She found him easy to talk to and their conversations as intellectually stimulating as they were entertaining. Equally enjoyable were the times when they didn't speak at all. The peacefulness of the hour and the shadowed darkness of her room added an intimacy to their time together, giving it an almost dreamlike quality.

During the short time she'd been in his home, they had developed a friendship of sorts, one that she had grown to cherish. They talked, laughed, watched television together. He'd even invited her to take a few walks with him—to the barn to check on a mare or to the front gate to collect the daily mail. She knew the short jaunts were his way of getting her out of the house for a while and away from the baby, something she was reluctant to do. To Addy, it was yet another indication of his thoughtfulness, his consideration.

"Look what I found?"

Addy jolted at the sound of Mack's voice, then turned to find him standing in the doorway, holding the baby.

She gave him a stern look. "Mack McGruder, if you woke that baby up, I'm going to be really mad."

"Didn't have to. He was already awake." Using the toe of his boot, he dragged a chair next to hers and dropped down, stretching out his legs, while he shifted the baby to cradle in the crook of one arm.

Addy watched, impressed at the ease with which he handled the infant.

"I'll bet you were a good father."

The thought was out of her mouth before she realized she'd spoken it out loud.

She laid a hand on his arm, regretting the thoughtless comment. "I'm sorry. It's just that you look so natural holding Johnny, so at ease."

He shook his head. "Being reminded I was a father doesn't bother me." He angled his head to look at her. "But I don't know that I was a good one. Sometimes it takes losing something before you realize how precious it is."

She nodded solemnly, thinking of all the regrets he might have, the if-I-could-only-do-it-overs he probably lived with every day. "What was your father like?" she asked impulsively.

He raised a brow, as if wondering where the question had come from, then shrugged. "Fun." Chuckling, he shook his head. "My mother swore that I could ride a horse before I could walk, and I imagine there was more truth in that statement than exaggeration. My father took me with him everywhere he went. Checking cattle, riding fence line, hunting, fishing." He shrugged again. "Whether it was work or play, he dragged me along."

Addy smiled, envying the relationship he'd described. "You were lucky."

"Yeah, I was," he agreed, then glanced her way. "What about your father? What was he like?"

"I never knew my dad. He was killed in Vietnam."

"That's tough," he said sympathetically.

She shrugged. "You can't miss what you never had."

"What about your stepfather? Were you close to him?"

"Which one?" she asked wryly.

He looked at her askance. "You have more than one?"

"Four to be exact."

His eyes rounded in amazement. "Four?"

"Yes, four. And, no, I wasn't close to any of them." She wrinkled her nose. "To be honest, the first three weren't around long enough for me to develop any kind of a relationship with them, and by the time the fourth came along, I really wasn't interested in trying."

"Four," he said again, as if having a hard time getting past that number.

She hesitated a moment, then figured he might as

well know her whole sordid past. "That's how many times my mother's been married. Four."

He frowned thoughtfully, as if mentally completing the steps to solve a complicated math problem, then gaped. "Your mother and father never—"

"No. They never married. When she told him she was pregnant, he ran off and joined the army, rather than make an honest woman of her. She's never forgiven him that slight."

He blew a silent whistle. "Well, that certainly explains some of the things she said on the phone."

"I can just imagine what all she had to say about my father. She never forgave Tony Rocci for what he did to her. And after he died, she shifted the blame to me."

"Well, that's just plain wrong," he said indignantly. "You can't be faulted for something you had no control over."

"Yeah? Well, try telling my mother that."

He stifled a shudder. "I think I'll pass." Frowning, he shifted the baby to his other arm. "Do you have any contact with your father's family?"

"No. My mother refused to have anything to do with the Roccis. I guess she blamed them for him abandoning her, as much as she did their son."

"But she gave you his name," he said in confusion.

"That wasn't a courtesy, I assure you. It was revenge. She wanted the world to know what a rotten SOB he was, that he'd gotten her pregnant, then skipped out on her."

He gave her a pointed look.

She drew back with a frown. "What?"

"Does this story sound at all familiar?"

She pursed her lips and looked away. "Parts of it maybe. But I'm nothing like my mother. I may detest your brother—"

"*Half* brother," he reminded her.

She flapped a hand. "Whatever. The only similarity between my mother's situation and mine is that we both got pregnant out of wedlock. I didn't give my baby his father's name, I gave him mine. Or would have," she added, and sent him a glance, "if you hadn't adopted him. And I will never blame Johnny for what happened. Getting pregnant was my fault and I accept full responsibility."

She dropped her gaze to the baby, and her face softened. "But I'll never regret having him," she said, and reached to take the infant from Mack. Cupping a hand at the back of the baby's head, she nuzzled his cheek with her nose. "How could I regret something as sweet as this?"

Settling back, she patted the baby absently, her thoughts growing reflective. "The weirdest thing happened the day I went into labor."

"A strange man showed up at your house?"

She shot him a look. "Besides that." Turning her gaze to the distance again, she frowned, remembering. "This lady called. She said that our fathers served together in Vietnam. Her call caught me totally off guard, because I seldom think about my father."

"I'd imagine it was a jolt to hear his name."

"Yeah. But what was weird was that she called to ask me about a piece of paper she found while going through her father's belongings. She wanted to know if my father had sent something similar to my mother."

"Did he?"

She lifted a shoulder. "Beats me. If he did and Mom kept it, it's probably in her trunk. When she moved to Hawaii, she left it in my garage. It's filled with all kinds of junk. Things she saved from her high school years, previous marriages, that kind of thing. Things she didn't want her husband to know she'd kept."

"If you know that's where you'd find it, why didn't you look?"

"I never had a chance. I went into labor." She slid her back down the chair, continuing to pat the baby's back, while letting her mind run with the possibilities. "Wouldn't it be something if it was valuable?" she said, thinking out loud. "I could get rid of my old sled and buy a new one."

"Sled?"

"My car. All that's holding it together are baling wire and duct tape."

He dropped his head back and laughed.

She gave him a quelling look, and he quickly sobered.

"Sorry," he murmured. "It was the duct tape and wire. I thought only country folk used that kind of stuff for repairs."

She jutted her chin. "Necessity and creativity know no boundaries."

He tipped his head, conceding the point. "No, I don't suppose they do."

She waved a hand. "Doesn't matter. It's foolish to put any hope in something that doesn't exist."

"You don't know that it doesn't," he reminded her. "It could be in the trunk."

"I doubt it. Even if he did send it to her, she wouldn't have kept it. She hated him. She wouldn't have wanted anything around that would remind her of him."

"He's smiling."

She blinked in confusion. "What?"

"The baby. He's smiling."

She lowered her son to her lap to see for herself. "He is!" she said in excitement, then laughed and lifted him to press a kiss on his cheek. "Johnny Mack, you are the sweetest baby ever," she cooed. "Your mommy loves you so much."

"Guess that makes it official," Mack said.

She looked at him in puzzlement. "What?"

He gestured at the baby. "You called him Johnny Mack. Makes it official."

Five

A woman could stand being waited on hand and foot just so long. After a month in Mack's house, Addy had reached her limit.

The kitchen was Zadie's domain, and she guarded it like a chicken would her eggs, refusing to allow Addy to so much as boil water. Mary, though much kinder when declining Addy's offers of help, was just as territorial about her household duties.

At first, Addy had enjoyed being spoiled, had considered the women's concern for her thoughtful, even sweet. Now it grated on her nerves, and she was determined to put an end to it before she went stark raving mad.

Thinking it best to discuss the situation with Mack before saying anything to the women, Addy went in search of him. Not finding him in his bedroom or office, she headed to the kitchen, where she found Zadie busily kneading dough. Steam rose from a large pot simmering on the stove, and the scent that emanated from it momentarily distracted her from her mission.

"What's cooking?" she asked, as she crossed to peer into the pot.

"Stew. Mr. Mack requested it special." Chuckling, Zadie rounded the island. "That man does like my stew."

Addy dipped her head over the pot and inhaled deeply. "I can see why. It smells delicious." She reached for the wooden spoon, intending to give it a quick stir.

Before she could, Zadie snatched the spoon from her hand.

"I does the cookin' 'round here," Zadie said, wagging the spoon in her face, like a stern finger, "not you."

Something in Addy snapped, and she snatched the spoon right back. "I'm the woman of this house and I can stir the damn stew anytime I want."

Zadie fell back a step, her eyes round as saucers, then flattened her lips. "Well, fine then," she said and returned to her dough. "Stir. But mind you do it gentle like," she warned. "Mr. Mack likes his taters in chunks, not shredded to bits."

Addy released a long, shaky breath, as surprised by her fit of temper as Zadie obviously was.

Dipping the spoon into the pot, she began to stir, careful to keep her strokes slow and easy.

Remembering her purpose in coming to the kitchen, she asked, "Where is Mack?"

"Don't know. Left 'bout an hour go. Got a call and took off like the devil hisself was chasing him."

Addy looked up in alarm. "Was something wrong?"

Zadie pushed a fist into the ball of dough, flattening it. "Didn't say. Just hung up the phone and lit out of here like his tail was on fire."

Addy's stomach knotted in dread. "Do you know who called?" she asked, trying to hide the fear in her voice.

Zadie pursed her lips and kept right on kneading. "Who Mr. Mack talks to is *his* business, ain't no business of mine."

Addy dropped the spoon, sure that she knew who the caller was. "It was Ty, wasn't it?"

"Ty Bodean?" With a humph, Zadie slapped the rolling pin down on the dough. "Mr. Mack wouldn't give that no-good boy the time of day. He done wore his welcome out here a long time ago. Always comin' 'round demandin' money." She humphed again. "Just like his daddy, that's what I says. But Mr. Mack made that promise to his mama, so he kept givin' it to 'im, knowin' as well I did that the boy would have it spent 'for he was out the door good." She shook her head sadly. "Went on for years till Mr. Mack finally got a stomachful of his foolishness and told him he wudn't gonna give him no more. Made Ty madder than a hornet, it did. Stormed outta here cussin' and yellin' and tellin' Mr. Mack how he'd get even with him."

"When?"

Zadie looked up, her brow pleated in confusion. "You mean about Ty leavin'?"

Addy nodded, not trusting her voice.

Zadie puckered her lips thoughtfully, then shrugged and went back to rolling out the dough. "Goin' on two years, I'd guess. Hadn't heard so much as his name mentioned 'round here, till the postmaster called and told Mr. Mack about those letters you sent. Stormed around for days, 'fore he decided he'd best do something 'fore Ty found hisself stuck with another paternity suit."

Her hands froze on the rolling pin and she glanced up, her expression stricken. "I didn't mean no disrespect, Miss Addy. Just 'cause Ty can't keep his zipper up, that ain't no reflection on you."

Even though she feared it was, Addy shook her head. "None taken."

Seemingly relieved, Zadie went back to rolling out the dough. "Marryin' you and bringin' you and the baby home with him wasn't what Mr. Mack had in mind that day he left for Dallas, and that's a fact. He was plannin' to pay you off, the same as he did the others." Chuckling, she set aside the rolling pin and wiped her palms down the front of her apron. "But I guess the Good Lord had somethin' else in mind for him this time around."

"What was that?"

Zadie looked up at her in surprise. "Why, Mr. Mack marryin' you and bringin' you and the baby back home with him, that's what." She picked up the biscuit cutter and sank it into the dough, frowning thoughtfully as she gave it a turn. "Now, I know it ain't none of my business," she began hesitantly. "But I think it's high time you was sharing Mr. Mack's bed. I know you had a hard time with the birth, and all. Mr. Mack tol' me about that. But that baby's a month old or more and you need to be doin' your duty to Mr. Mack and not sleepin' in that room by yourself."

Addy stared, stunned by Zadie's suggestion, then turned and all but ran for the door, her cheeks flaming in embarrassment.

"Where you goin' in such a rush?" Zadie called after her. "I thought you was gonna stir that stew?"

Anxious to show Addy the surprise he'd bought for her, Mack tossed his hat onto the kitchen counter. "Hey, Zadie. Where's Addy?"

Scowling, Zadie slammed the oven door. "How would I know?" she snapped, tossing up her hands. "Nobody tells me nothin', jist zip in and outta my kitchen like they was bees chasin' honey."

Mack lifted a brow, surprised by her sour mood. "If you're upset with me because I didn't tell you where I was going, I'm sorry. I was in hurry. Had some business in town I needed to take care of."

She spun to face him and planted her hands on her hips. "Did I ask you where you was?" Before he could answer, she marched to the refrigerator, her nose in the air, and yanked open the door. "Everybody askin' where everybody else is," she muttered under her breath, as she dug around inside. "A person would think I's a secretary instead of the cook."

When she turned from the refrigerator and nearly bumped into Mack, she scowled again. "I thought you was in an all-fired hurry to find Miss Addy." She pushed out a hand, shooing him away. "Well, get on with you. I've got dinner to cook."

Deciding it was safer to leave than question her further, he went in search of Addy. He found her in her bedroom, standing before the French doors, staring out.

"Addy?"

She jumped but didn't turn around. "Yes?" she said uneasily.

He noticed that she was wringing her hands and wondered if it had anything to do with Zadie's sour mood.

"Did you and Zadie have an argument or something?" he asked.

She tensed. "Did she say that we did?"

He bit down on his frustration, wondering if the women in the house had conspired during his absence to drive him crazy. "No. But she nearly bit my head off when I asked her where you were."

"What else did she tell you?"

Puzzled, he shook his head. "Nothing. Just chased me out of her kitchen."

She turned then, and he saw the tears that brimmed in her eyes.

"What's wrong?" he asked in concern.

"It's my fault she's in a bad mood. I yelled at her. Zadie," she clarified, then sniffed and dragged a hand beneath her nose. "I just wanted to stir the stew, and she snatched the spoon away from me, and I...I—" She lifted her hands, then let them drop helplessly to her sides, tears welling in her eyes again. "Something inside me just snapped. I'm so bored," she said miserably. "Nobody will let me do anything. Zadie. Mary. They treat me like I'm an invalid or an idiot, and I don't know which is worse."

"They just don't want you to overdo."

"Overdo?" she repeated, her tears instantly drying. "Much more of this sedentary lifestyle and I'll atrophy! I'm used to being busy. At home and at work. Eight-hour shifts of nonstop action in an Emergency Room in no way prepares a person for this kind of in-activity. Much more and I'm going to go crazy."

"Do you want me to talk to them?"

"Yes. No." Groaning, she dropped her face to her hands. "I don't know. I just want to do something, *any*thing, and they won't let me."

Though it was a struggle, Mack managed not to laugh. "I'll talk to them. Tell them to let you help when you want."

She dropped her hands, her face stricken. "Promise you won't tell them that I said anything. I mean... well—" She began to wring her hands again. "They've been so nice to me. I don't want them to think I'm un-grateful."

He drew a cross over his heart. "You have my word. They'll never know this discussion took place."

She sagged her shoulders. "Thank you."

Hiding a smile, he draped an arm around her and headed her for the door. "Come outside with me. I want to show you something."

She hung back, her gaze on the nursery door behind them. "But what if Johnny Mack wakes up?"

He urged her on. "There are monitors all over the house. Mary or Zadie will tend to him if he does."

When they reached the front porch, he stopped. "Well?" he asked, indicating the vehicle parked on the drive. "What do you think?"

She stared, her jaw going slack, then whipped her gaze to his. "You bought a new car? But you already have a Mercedes and a truck. What do you need with another vehicle?"

Before he could explain that the car was for her, she took off at a run. When he caught up with her, she was behind the wheel, her head tipped back against the leather headrest, her eyes closed.

She inhaled deeply, her expression rapturous. "Smell that? New car. Nothing in the world compares."

Chuckling, he circled the hood and climbed into the passenger seat.

Flipping open her eyes, she leaned forward to examine the controls. "Oh, my gosh. Satellite Radio! That is beyond awesome."

"So you like the car?"

"Like it?" She sank back against the seat with a dramatic sigh. "This is the original lustmobile."

He dug the keys from his pocket and offered them to her. "Give it a try."

She tucked her hands beneath her thighs. "Uh-uh. No way. What if I wrecked it?"

"Don't worry. It's insured." He nudged the key against her arm. "Go on. Try it out."

Worrying her lip, she eyed the key like a druggie

would his next fix, then snatched it from his hand. "Okay. But if I wreck it, it's your fault."

She started the engine, then fell back against the seat, her body limp. "Oh, my God," she said weakly. "I don't think I can stand it."

"Stand what?"

"It started on the first try."

Laughing, Mack pulled the seat belt across his chest and clicked it into place. "I take it the sled doesn't."

She rolled her head to the side and gave him a bland look. "I'm lucky if it starts at all."

"Well, you won't have to worry about that anymore," he assured her.

She snorted a laugh. "Yeah, right. The sled has to last a couple more years, at the least."

Mack laid a hand on her arm. "This is yours, Addy."

She stared, her face going slack. "Mine?"

He laughed. "Yes, yours."

She switched off the ignition and shook her head. "I can't accept something like this."

"Why not? You need something to drive."

"Well, yeah. But I've got my sled."

"Which is in Dallas," he reminded her.

She opened her arms, indicating the car. "But I can't afford something like this."

"Yes, you can. I told you. I'm a wealthy man."

She shook her head again. "You may be, but I'm not."

"You're my wife," he reminded her. "What's mine is yours."

She stared, eyes wide, then gulped. "You mean you're just…giving this to me?"

"Seems like." Smiling, he reached to turn the key. "Now how about taking us for a ride?"

Later that night Addy lay in bed listening to the sounds coming from the nursery. The wooden creak of the rocking chair; the low, husky rumble of Mack's voice as he talked to Johnny Mack. Any minute now she knew he would be bringing the baby to her to feed. She could've easily climbed from her bed and saved him the trip, but she hated to deny him this special time with Johnny Mack when he seemed to enjoy it so much.

So she lay there listening, while Mack carried on a one-sided conversation with her son, and let her thoughts drift back over the day.

She still couldn't believe Mack had bought her a car. And not just any car, she thought with a shiver of excitement. A Lexus SUV. How had he known that was the vehicle she'd always wanted, the one she'd lusted over, dreamed of owning? To her, it was the perfect mommy car. Luxurious enough to satisfy even the most discriminating woman's need for extravagance, yet roomy and durable enough to use for driving carpools and hauling groceries. It was the perfect car for a family.

Family?

She stared wide-eyed, considering. But that's exactly what she had begun to think of them as, she realized. A family. She knew it was wrong for her to think of them as such. It wasn't at all the arrangement she had made with Mack. He had offered her a marriage of convenience, without any sexual or emotional obligations, a name for her baby. So why would she allow herself think of them as a family, when it was clear that wasn't what Mack had wanted or what she had agreed to?

Growing pensive, she glanced toward the nursery. She couldn't see Mack and the baby, but she could hear the creak of the rocker, Mack's low crooning, and knew they were there in the darkness. Did he think of them as a family? she wondered. He was definitely crazy about Johnny Mack, spent as much time with the baby as he possibly could. And he seemed to genuinely like Addy. He was kind to her, generous, thoughtful. But he seldom touched her. Not like a husband would his wife. He treated her more like a…a sister or perhaps a close friend.

You need to be doin' your duty to Mr. Mack and not sleepin' in that room by yourself.

Heat crawled up her neck as she remembered Zadie's comment. What on earth would possess Zadie to say such a thing? Surely she knew that Mack and Addy's marriage wasn't a real one, not in the traditional sense. Heavens, how could she *not* know? Mack and Addy had been strangers prior to him coming to Dallas. And they'd married less than forty-eight hours after they'd met! Strangers didn't marry for love—those kinds of feelings developed over time—and Addy wouldn't sleep with a man she didn't love…or at least think she was in love with.

And duty? She rolled her eyes. She would *never* sleep with a man out of any sense of duty. There had to be something stronger before she'd ever consider giving herself to a man. She had to *feel* something for him, an emotion, a connection of some kind. Definitely something more than a sense of duty.

The rocker creaked to a stop, and she mentally slammed the door on her thoughts, knowing that Mack would be bringing her the baby. Hearing the pad of his feet on the carpet, she quickly scooted up to a sitting position and held out her arms. "Is he hungry?" she asked, forcing a smile.

He leaned to give her the baby. "Starving."

Chuckling, she looked down at her son and arranged her nightgown for him to nurse. "He's turning into a little pig."

Yawning, Mack stretched out across the foot of her bed. "He's definitely putting on some weight."

She folded back the blanket to trail a finger down a dimpled thigh. "Three, maybe four pounds would be my guess."

"Bill can tell us for sure when we take him to his appointment tomorrow."

She glanced up in surprise. "You made Johnny Mack a doctor's appointment?"

"Yeah. I saw Bill in town this afternoon, or rather yesterday afternoon," he corrected, with a glance at his wristwatch. "He said we could bring him in around noon, if that's all right with you."

She looked down at the baby and swallowed hard, knowing he would be receiving his first series of shots and dreading it for him. "He won't hurt him, will he?"

He choked a laugh. "Bill's been taking care of babies for years. He knows what he's doing."

She tucked the blanket protectively around Johnny Mack's legs. "I know. It's just that—"

"He's your baby," he finished for her.

She gave him a sheepish look. "You probably think I'm one of those crazy, overprotective mothers."

"No, I think you're a mother who loves her son very much. There's nothing wrong with that."

She started to reply, but a cramp knotted in her foot. "Ow," she cried and drew up her knee.

Mack pushed up higher on his elbow. "What's wrong?"

With the baby in her arms, it was impossible for her to reach her foot, so she kicked her leg free from the covers and flexed her toes hard. "I've got a cramp."

"Here. Let me."

He gripped her foot between his hands, pressed his thumb deeply into the arch and began massaging. After a few minutes the cramp began to ease.

"Better?" he asked.

"Yes," she said in relief. "Thank you."

He sank back down to his elbow again, but kept a hand curved around her foot, his fingers stroking up and down its length.

He didn't seem conscious of the action, but Addy was. Heat radiated up her leg, gathered in her stomach.

She knew she should break the contact, but she couldn't. The silky glide of his fingers was mesmerizing, sensual, erotic. The heat that had gathered in her stomach churned hot and molten, climbing higher and higher until it parched her mouth, burned behind her eyes. She was aroused, she realized slowly, and was stunned that Mack could bring her to such a level with something as simple as a foot massage.

She stole a glance at him and was relieved that the shadowed darkness kept him from seeing her face clearly and possibly knowing her thoughts. She knew it was crazy, insane, but the desire to make love with him was there in her mind, a yearning that throbbed deep in her womb.

"We could grab a bite to eat after we see Bill," Mack said, continuing the conversation. "Give you an opportunity to see a little bit more of Lampasas."

She stared, wondering how he could talk about something as mundane as lunch, when all she could think about was undressing him. Did he not *feel* what she was feeling, *want* what she wanted? How could he *not,* when it was all she could do to breathe?

Because he wasn't attracted to her.

The answer was so obvious and so brutally humbling, it was like having cold water thrown in the face.

And why would he be attracted to her? she asked herself miserably. She'd just given birth. She still had a good ten pounds to lose, her breasts were as big as melons and her scent—if she had one—was Eau de Baby. What man in his right mind would find her in the least bit alluring?

Disheartened, she eased her foot from his grip and lifted the baby to her shoulder to burp.

"I don't know," she said evasively. "Maybe we should wait and see how Johnny Mack feels after he gets his shots."

* * *

Bill appeared in the doorway to the reception area and waved them back. Since Mack had the baby, Addy was left to gather up the diaper bag and her purse and follow.

By the time she reached the exam room, Bill had the baby and was cooing to him. He glanced up as she entered. "Hey, Addy. How are you feeling?"

His warm smile put her immediately at ease. "Fine, thank you."

"Have you had your checkup yet?"

She shook her head. "No. I thought I'd go to Dallas and see my own doctor."

"Why wait?" Bill plucked the phone from its cradle on the wall.

"Oh, no, really," she said, panicking at the thought of being examined by a stranger. "That's not ne—"

Bill held up a finger. "Hey, Sally," he said into the receiver. "Mack and Addy are here with the baby. Do you think Kathy could squeeze Addy in for a postpartum exam?" He listened a moment, then nodded. "Good. I'll send her right over."

He hung up the phone and turned to Addy. "Kathy—she's my wife, by the way, and a darn good OB-GYN—can see you right now, if you hurry." With the baby cradled in the crook of one arm, he opened the door and pointed to a second set of doors at the end of the hall. "Right through there," he said. "Just tell Sally—the lady behind the reception desk—that you're Addy, and she'll fix you right up."

"But what about Johnny Mack?" Addy shot a terri-fied look at Mack. "I can't just leave him."

Mack placed a hand at the small of her back and urged her out the door. "Don't worry about Johnny Mack. I'll be here with him."

"But, Mack—"

"Better hurry," Bill warned. "Kathy runs a tight ship. Put her behind schedule and she gets in a hell of a mood."

Before Addy could argue further, the door closed in her face.

Following the physical portion of her exam, Addy followed Sally to the doctor's office, thinking that having a female OB-GYN wasn't such a bad idea. She'd felt more comfortable and a whole lot less self-conscious being examined by a woman than she ever had with Dr. Wharton.

As she took a seat opposite the doctor's desk, the office door opened and Kathy strode in.

"Everything looked fine," she reported, as she sat down behind her desk. "The stitches from the episiot-omy have all dissolved and the incision has healed nicely." She flipped open the file the nurse had left on her desk and scanned the lab reports. "Blood count looks good," she said. "Iron level more than sufficient." She closed the file and beamed a smile at Addy. "I'd say you're good to boogie."

Addy blinked. "Excuse me?"

Chuckling, Kathy sank back in her chair. "Sorry. I'll translate. You can resume your normal sexual activities."

Heat crawled up Addy's neck. "Oh. Well…I, uh… Mack and I…well, you see…"

Kathy did her best to hide a smile. "I'm not saying that you have to have sex tonight. I'm merely telling you that you're physically ready, if the situation should present itself."

If possible, Addy's face heated even more. "Yes. Right. Of course."

Smiling openly now, Kathy stood and extended her hand. "It's been a pleasure meeting you, Addy. You're everything Mack said you were and more."

Addy gaped. "Mack talked to you about me?"

Kathy rounded her desk to escort Addy to the door. "Not directly. But Mack and Bill have been joined at the hip since they were kids. If something is going on in one's life, the other knows about it." She stopped in the doorway and shrugged. "What Bill knows, I know. The man couldn't keep a secret if his life depended on it." She gave Addy an assessing look, then nodded. "And I have to agree. You're perfect."

You're perfect.

Addy played Kathy's comment over and over through her mind as she folded the clothes Mary had laundered, trying to figure out what the woman had meant. Since Kathy had just confessed that Bill told her everything, she had to assume that by "I agree" it was Bill she agreed with. But about what? she asked herself in confusion.

"How's he feeling?"

Addy jumped at the sound of Mack's voice and turned to find him in the doorway. Unbidden, another of Kathy's comments popped into her mind…her verdict of "you're good to boogie."

Mortified that she would think of *that,* she whipped her head back around, praying her cheeks weren't as red as they felt. "Fine," she said, and gulped to steady her voice. "He hasn't had any fever or been fussy."

Mack crossed the room to peek into the nursery where the baby slept. Her heart hammering in her chest, Addy watched him through the corner of her eye, wondering why, more and more often, her thoughts seemed to turn to sex whenever he was near. Six months ago she wouldn't have given him a second look. Older men were a turnoff for her, and Mack was at least ten years her senior. He failed in the physical department, too, as she was usually drawn to taller, lankier men, and though there was no question that Mack was tall—a good six feet, if not more—he definitely wasn't lanky. He was built more like a brick wall—and about as impregnable as one. From day one, he'd been bossy to the point of overbearing, and that was a relationship killer in her book, as she tended to bow her back when told what to do.

He turned away from the nursery, and she quickly busied herself folding clothes, so he wouldn't catch her staring.

"He looks like he weathered the shots okay," he said, as he moved to stand beside her.

"I thought so, too."

He picked up a bib and rubbed a thumb over the teddy bear appliqué on its front. "Did you enjoy having lunch in town yesterday?"

She glanced his way, surprised that he'd ask when she specifically remembered telling him she had, as well as thanking him for the meal. "Yes. I told you I did."

Nodding, he dropped the bib and picked up a bootie and slipped two fingers inside. "What do you think of Lampasas?"

Though he was obviously talking to her, he didn't look at her, which struck her as odd. He kept his gaze on the bootie and the puppetlike movements he was making with his fingers.

"It's nice," she replied, frowning slightly. "Much smaller than Dallas, but small towns have their own special charm." Unable to stem her curiosity, she asked bluntly, "Why all the questions?"

With a shrug he tossed the bootie back into the basket and turned away. "No reason. Just curious."

Addy stared after him, as bewildered by his questions as she was by his obvious reluctance to meet her gaze.

It was hormonal.

Addy had reached the conclusion during the night, while unable to sleep. It was the only explanation she could come up with that made any sense for her sudden attraction to Mack. She knew hormonal changes were common in pregnant women, both during and after a pregnancy. She'd experienced a few herself while carrying Johnny Mack. The sudden, unexplainable rush of tears; the drastic swings in her internal thermostat, leaving her freezing cold one minute and sweating profusely the next.

Hormones, she thought decisively. That had to be it.

She stole a glance at Mack, sitting opposite her at the table, his attention on the folded newspaper propped beside his plate. He'd barely acknowledged her presence when she had joined him at the table for breakfast, and had kept his gaze fixed on the newspaper throughout the meal.

Grimacing, she stabbed her fork into a triangle of pancake. It wasn't fair, she thought miserably, as she dragged it through the puddle of syrup on her plate. Why should she suddenly be stricken with an acute attack of lust, while his interest in her seemed to be dwindling with each passing day?

Not that he ever had been interested, she thought glumly. But he'd at least been nicer to her, more friendly. Keeping her company at night while she fed the baby. Sitting with her in the evening and watching TV. Insisting she take walks with him to the barns where he stabled his horses or to the pastures to see his cattle, in order to get her out of the house for a while and away from the baby.

She stole another look at him and felt the now-familiar stir of desire in her womb. The streaks of gray at his temples were nothing if not sexy. And the creases at the corner of his eyes and those between his brows when he concentrated, added an air of sophistication to an already handsome face. And that chest… She covered her mouth with her napkin to smother a lustful moan, imagining what it would be like to have it bare beneath her hands, pressed against her breasts.

"Mr. Mack?"

At the sound of Zadie's voice, Addy snatched her napkin from her mouth and balled it guiltily in her lap.

"Yes?" Mack replied to Zadie, his gaze still on his newspaper.

"I gonna need a couple days off."

He lifted his head to peer at her, his forehead creased in concern. "Is there a problem?"

She twisted her hands in her apron. "It's my sister Mabel. Her boy Willie just called. Said Mabel fell and broke her leg last night."

He set the newspaper down, giving her his full attention. "I'm sorry to hear that. Is she going to be all right?"

She gulped, nodded. "They put in a steel pin to hold it together. Done the surgery early this morning. But I needs to go and tend to her. Make sure she don't overdo none."

Mack nodded gravely. "Stay as long as you need. Do you want me to drive you?"

"I 'preciate that, but I can drive myself." She wrung her hands. "I jest hate to up and leave y'all so sudden like. If I'd know'd, I'd've cooked up a bunch of food to see y'all through till I get back."

Mack glanced at Addy. "I'm sure Addy wouldn't mind doing a little cooking."

Addy brightened at the suggestion. "Not at all. I love to cook."

"I suppose she could handle things," Zadie said doubtfully. "I could leave some recipes for her to follow."

Mack rose and placed a hand on Zadie's shoulder. "Don't you worry about us. It's Mabel you need to concern yourself with. Addy will see that we don't starve."

Addy stood before the mirror in her bathroom, naked as the day she was born, giving her body a last brutal assessment. Her face appeared somewhat thinner, she decided, her waist more defined, her stomach almost as flat as it had been before she had become pregnant. She cupped her hands beneath her breasts and tipped her head to the side to study them. They were definitely bigger than her prepregnant state, but they had lost that "melon" look and appeared almost…well, normal.

Relieved, she leaned close to examine her face and smoothed a finger over her cheek, searching for the dark spot that had appeared several months ago, "pregnancy mask" as Dr. Wharton had referred to it. She was pleased to find that it had faded, and knew that with a little makeup it wouldn't be noticeable at all.

Stepping back, she lowered her gaze to look at her abdomen and spotted a couple of stretch marks. Wincing, she traced a nail over the most obvious one that lay along her bikini line, then sputtered a laugh. Bikini line, she thought, rolling her eyes. As if she'd be caught dead in a bikini, postpregnancy or not.

Telling herself that a couple of stretch marks were small payment for the gift of her son, she stepped into the tub and, with a sigh, slid into the chin-deep bubbles.

Lined along the edge of the tub were everything she'd need to make herself beautiful…or, at the very least, presentable. A razor and shaving cream, an avocado mask for her face, perfumed oils to scent her body, lavender bath salts to help her relax. Frowning, she sprinkled the salts generously over the water, knowing she was going to need all the help she could get in the relaxation department.

As she'd discovered, planning a seduction was hell on a woman's nerves.

The idea to seduce Mack had come to her shortly after Mary had left at five o'clock and with her departure the realization that, with Mary gone for the day and Zadie in Austin taking care of her sister, Addy and Mack would have the house to themselves for the first time ever—with the exception of Johnny Mack, of course, but she had already put him down for the night and was praying he would sleep until morning.

Although the idea had come unbidden and in a flash of what could only be described as divine inspiration, she hadn't embraced it immediately. She'd stewed and fretted, worrying that Mack wouldn't find her physically attractive. After a good ten minutes of hand wringing, she'd decided to hell with it. What makeup and candlelight couldn't hide, she wouldn't worry about. He'd accept her as she was or not all. No big deal.

Yeah, right, she thought wryly.

Ignoring the tremble in her fingers, she smeared the mask over her face and let it set while she lathered and shaved her legs. Next came a full-body scrub with the loofah sponge and the scented oils, followed by a brisk shampoo and conditioner for her hair.

Once she was sure her hair was clean, her body smooth and seductively scented, she stepped from the bath. After drying off, she looked around for her clothes and hissed a breath when she realized she'd forgotten to bring them in with her.

With a sigh of resignation, she wrapped the towel around her and opened the bathroom door, tucking the ends to secure the towel between her breasts. Halfway across the room, she heard a noise behind her and glanced over her shoulder to find Mack backing from the nursery. Her heart skipped a beat, then kicked hard against the wall of her chest. She looked toward the closet, then back at the bathroom, mentally calculating the distance to each…and realized she'd never make it to either without being seen.

Standing with a damp towel draped around her, her hair hanging in wet clumps to her shoulders, her face freshly scrubbed, but minus the concealing makeup she'd intended to apply, she could all but see her plans for a seduction going up in smoke before her very eyes.

Mack turned. "Hey," he said, smiling. "I was just about to—" He stopped short, his smile melting as he slid his gaze slid down her front. "You're wearing a towel," he said dully, then lifted his gaze to hers.

She jerked up her chin, refusing to let her embarrassment show. "I forgot to take my clothes into the bathroom with me."

His gaze skimmed down her front again, and his Adam's apple bobbed convulsively. When he lifted his eyes to meet hers a second time, she saw the heat that burned there, would swear she felt it sizzle and pop against her damp skin.

Praying she wasn't reading him wrong, she inhaled deeply…and dropped the towel.

Six

It wasn't until the towel hit the floor that Addy remembered candlelight and the fact that she'd been counting on it, as well as the makeup, to conceal some of the flaws on her body. Thankfully, the overhead light was off, but the bedside lamp wasn't, which meant Mack had a fairly clear view of her every imperfection, if he were to look closely enough.

And he was definitely looking.

At the moment, his gaze was riveted on her breasts. Though she wanted more than anything to grab the towel and make a run for it, she squared her shoulders and thrust out her chin.

She heard what she thought was a moan come from him, and a shiver of response skated down her spine. *In for a penny, in for a pound,* she told herself, and forced herself to take that first bold step.

His gaze shot to hers. "Addy…"

She heard the warning in his voice…or was it a plea? Praying it was the latter, she stopped in front of him and laid her hand on his chest. She felt him jolt at her touch, the thunder of his heart beneath her palm, but his gaze remained steady on hers, his eyes turning a dark, smoldering blue.

"Do you know what you're doing?"

This time the warning in his tone was clear. She gulped, nodded. "Yes."

His chest swelled beneath her palm as he hauled in a breath, then deflated, as he released it. "You have exactly two seconds to change your mind."

She lifted a brow in challenge. "And if I don't?"

"One…two."

Before she had time to draw a breath, his mouth came down on hers, fierce and demanding, his arms wrapping around her like a vise. She felt the need in him, tasted it, even as a part of her mind marveled that she had the power to evoke that level of emotion in a man.

His hands burned like brands on her back, searing her flesh, as he forced her body up hard against his. She felt the swell of his erection against her abdomen, the heat of it spreading through her in wave after dizzying wave, and wondered why she'd waited so long to seduce him.

He was a marvelous kisser. She was surprised she still had the presence of mind to form the thought. His lips were possessive, demanding, arousing, as were the hands that stroked her bare back, urging her ever closer. When her breath began to burn in her lungs, her knees to grow weak, he slowly softened the kiss, his impatience giving way to a sensual exploration she found no less arousing.

The desire to touch him, to have her hands on his bare skin, as his were on hers, was too strong to ignore any longer.

"Your clothes," she said breathlessly, and reached for the buttons of his shirt.

Though he loosened his hold on her enough to give her access, he kept his arms looped low on her waist, holding her groin against his. She'd released three when she sensed his gaze. She glanced up and found him looking at her, his expression…curious? Questioning? Confused?

Unsure, she stilled her hands, fearing she'd done something wrong. "What?"

Shaking his head, he dipped his head to nuzzle her neck. "Nothing."

Though his reply did nothing to allay the doubts that suddenly crowded her mind, his mouth did the trick, as he nibbled his way up her neck and over her chin. She freed the last button on his shirt, just as he found her mouth again. Her breath stolen, she braced her hands against his chest, as much to steady herself as to satisfy her need to touch him. Warmth, strength…she sensed both beneath her palms, as she swept them up his chest and over his shoulders to strip away his shirt.

With a groan he cupped her buttocks and brought her up hard against him. "Bed."

His request was one-word simple, leaving no doubt in her mind as to his meaning, his needs. Before she could tell him that's what she'd had in mind from the start, he scooped her up into his arms.

She might've shivered deliciously at his caveman tactics, perhaps even lifted a brow at the finesse with which he stripped back the bedcovers while holding her in his arms. But she had time for neither, as he immediately began to undress.

Lying on her back in the center of her bed, she followed his movements like a voyeur, watching as he toed off his boots and peeled down his jeans. But when he straightened, her gaze refused to budge from the stiff shaft jutting from a nest of dark hair at the juncture of his legs. She didn't want to compare. That seemed so tawdry, so high schoolish. But she couldn't help but notice that he was better equipped than Ty. Gulping, she lifted her gaze to his.

With his eyes fixed on hers, he sank a knee into the mattress and stretched out over her, until his mouth covered hers again. His body was like a blanket, warm and comforting, his kiss so tender, so gentle, it drew tears to her eyes.

He lifted his head and combed her hair back to search her face, saw her tears. "It's okay for us to do this, isn't it?" he asked hesitantly.

She didn't need for him to tell her what he meant by *this*. She gulped, nodded. "According to Kathy, I'm good to boogie."

He blinked, then hooted a laugh and fell to his back at her side. "God, that sounds just like her."

She felt a moment's panic, fearing that she'd somehow ruined the mood by telling him what Kathy had said. But then his gaze slid to her breasts and his smile slowly faded. He rolled to his side and reached to cup one in the palm of his hand, his expression soft.

"When I'd watch you nurse Johnny Mack, I'd wonder what your breasts looked like, how they might feel." He rubbed the ball of his thumb over the nipple, then leaned to flick his tongue over the budded tip and said, "How they'd taste."

Prickles of desire danced to life beneath her skin at his tongue's urging, and shot to quiver like plucked strings in her womb. Trembling, she squeezed her knees together, fearing she would come apart right then and there.

He glanced up, and she saw that the heat had returned to his eyes. Holding her in place with nothing more than his gaze, he pushed up to an elbow and pressed his lips to hers. A shiver shook her, as he hooked an arm around her neck and pulled her over on top of him, holding her face to his between his broad hands. He deepened the kiss by degrees, while shifting his hands to stroke up and down her back. Heat radiated from her, beading her skin, slicking her hands. Sure that he intended to drive her mad before he made love to her, she rocked her hips impatiently against his.

His response was to grip her buttocks firmly within his hands, holding her against him. He thrust his tongue between her lips, an oral teasing that shot heat through her, a bolt of lightning that blinded and seared. Never in her life had she experienced anything like this, she thought desperately. Never such urgency, such need.

"I want you," she whispered, pressing herself against him.

He drew back to look at her, his expression uncertain. "I don't want to hurt you."

"You won't," she told him, even as she slipped a hand between their bodies to guide him to her. The tip of his erection slid across her opening, and she nearly wept in frustration.

"Mack," she gasped, straining toward him.

He tightened his hands on her buttocks to still her. "Easy," he murmured. "Let's take this slow."

She shook her head wildly. "No. Please. *Now.*"

In spite of her demand for urgency, he entered her slowly, inch by slow inch. The tremble of his hands on her hips, the quiver of his legs against hers, told her how much his restraint cost him. Though touched by his concern for her, she didn't want slow. What she wanted, needed, was *him.*

Pushing up to her knees, she clamped her legs at his hips. "You can't hurt me," she told him again, as she lowered her hips to his groin. Taking him in to his hilt, she dropped her head back with a groan, glorying in the sheer, sensual pleasure of having him fill her completely, of feeling his hips ground against hers. After a moment, she began to rock slowly back and forth, absorbing each sensation, while the pressure built inside her.

She felt the change in his body, even as her own body readied. The gathering and bunching of muscle, the quiver of flesh, the almost desperate dig of his fingers into her buttocks. Wanting, needing to share that ultimate experience with him, she braced her hands against his chest and thrust her hips back hard against his groin. She held herself there, on that pinnacle of pleasure, her head thrown back, her lungs heaving, accepting the gift of his passion, while her body exploded around him with her own.

Until that moment she'd never truly understood the meaning of rapture, what it was to experience it firsthand. But she knew now. The pleasure, the intensity of it, was blinding, liberating, spellbinding, humbling.

She drew in a breath through her nostrils, held it a moment, then opened her eyes and released it on a sigh...and found Mack watching her, his eyes a soft, translucent blue. His face was damp with perspiration, a dark stubble shadowed his jaw. With his gaze on hers, he reached up to stroke a hand over her belly, and a soft smile curved his lips.

She tensed, remembering the stretch mark that trailed along her bikini line. Wishing she could melt into the mattress or, at the very least, switch off the bedside lamp, she placed a hand over her stomach, trying to hide it.

"Don't," he scolded gently. "That's nothing to be ashamed of."

As if to prove it, he hitched himself up on an elbow, then bent his head to press a kiss against the mark. Lifting his head, he met her gaze, as he dragged his thumb through the moisture he'd left there. "That's a medal of motherhood. Wear it with pride."

Her heart seemed to stop a moment, then kicked against her ribs. She was falling in love with him, she realized, as she stared into his eyes. How could she feel anything less for a man who could say such an outrageously sweet thing and obviously mean it?

Before she had time to completely absorb the notion, consider it, he caught her arms and pulled her down to his chest. Their faces only inches apart, he searched her gaze.

"Addy..."

He caught her face between his hands and drew it down to touch his lips to hers. The kiss was so tender, so incredibly sweet, it brought tears to her eyes.

Drawing back, he swept a finger across her damp lashes. "Hey," he said softly. "Why the tears?"

She gulped, shook her head. "I...I don't know."

"I didn't hurt you, did I?"

She shook her head again, then tucked her face into the curve of his neck. "No. I'm fine."

Cupping a hand at the back of her head, he pressed his lips to her hair. "Regrets?"

She sputtered a watery laugh. "How can I regret something I planned?"

He drew back to search her face. "You planned this?"

Realizing how awful she must look, she touched a hand to her hair and grimaced. "Well, not *this* exactly. I had it all thought out. Candlelight. Soft music. A bottle of wine. A totally irresistible *me*." She wrinkled her nose. "Unfortunately you caught me before the transformation was complete."

"I don't know about that." He swept her hair back from her face, held it there. "I wasn't able to resist you."

He lifted his head and touched his lips to hers. "You knocked me completely off my feet." Dipping his head, he nuzzled her neck, then inhaled deeply. "What's that scent you're wearing?"

She closed her eyes and arched her neck, giving him better access. "Seduction. It seemed appropriate."

Zadie would have a fit if she could see her kitchen. Cracked eggshells littered the island, a pound of bacon lay in a heap beside the range ready to add to the skillet warming there, and flour dusted every surface within a five-foot span of the dough board where biscuits were lined up like soldiers preparing for battle.

But Addy didn't care about the mess she'd made. What Zadie couldn't see couldn't hurt her, and Addy was having the time of her life.

She'd spent an unbelievable night in bed with Mack, making love, cuddling and finally sleeping, only to wake and do it all again. And now, while he showered, she was cooking his breakfast, which she considered the perfect way to celebrate what had proven to be an unforgettable night.

And if her stomach was a little jittery about facing him in the bright light of day, she supposed that was to be expected. It was one thing to make wild, passionate love with a man in the dark of night, and quite another to sit across the breakfast table from him afterward and share a meal she'd prepared, as if nothing had changed between them.

"Smells good."

She jumped, nearly burning her hand on the skillet, then wilted, as Mack looped his arms around her waist from behind and buried his nose in the curve of her neck.

"Me or what's cooking?" she asked coyly.

Chuckling, he nipped her neck, then moved to stand beside her, keeping an arm looped at her waist. "Both. What's for breakfast?"

"Biscuits, omelets and bacon. Hungry?"

"As a bear." He gave her bottom a playful pat and turned away. "I checked on Johnny Mack," he said, as he crossed to the refrigerator. "He's still asleep." He poured orange juice into glasses and brought one to her. Sliding an arm around her waist again, he rested his hip against hers and sipped his juice, while she fried bacon.

To Addy the whole scene screamed family. In fact, if it were any more so, she feared she would explode with happiness.

"What have you got planned for today?" he asked.

She lifted a shoulder as she turned the bacon. "Nothing special. Do a few loads of laundry. Maybe help Mary around the house. What about you?"

"I need to go into town and take care of some business. Later I thought we might do something. Just the two of us. I bet Mary would jump at the chance to babysit Johnny Mack."

She looked up at him in surprise. "You mean, like a date?"

His smile sheepish, he rubbed a hand across the back of his neck. "Yeah. Something like that. Marriage first, then lovers. Somewhere along the way, seems we missed a step or two."

Addy spent an insane amount of time agonizing over what to wear on her "date" with Mack. It wasn't as if she needed to impress him, she told herself, as she flipped through the closet for the third time, searching for something appropriate to wear. He'd seen her at her absolute worst more times than she cared to think about, and he hadn't run yet, so what difference did it make what she wore?

"Because it's our first date," she reminded herself, "and I want everything to be perfect." She pulled a sundress from the closet and held it up to her, as she crossed to the bed. "What do you think?" she asked the baby, who sat propped up in an infant carrier on her bed. "Too casual? Too revealing?"

Johnny Mack kicked his feet and cooed, obviously excited at the attention he was receiving.

"So you think I'd look good in this, huh?" Laughing, she bent to drop a kiss on his cheek. "You're just saying that because I'm your mommy."

Straightening, she held up the dress, frowning as she studied her reflection in the dresser mirror. "Okay," she conceded. "I'll wear it." She glanced toward the baby and raised a brow in warning. "But if Mack doesn't go all google-eyed when he sees me in it, the blame is all yours."

In answer, Johnny Mack blew a bubble of spit.

Laughing, Addy bussed him another kiss. "You are just too darn cute."

Addy crossed and uncrossed her legs for the third time since they'd left the house.

"Did I tell Mary that I left bottles of breast milk in the refrigerator?"

"Twice," Mack replied patiently, then reached to pat her hand. "He'll be fine. Mary has four kids of her own. She knows how to take care of a baby."

She caught her lower lip between her teeth. "But her children are older, aren't they? She may have forgotten that she needs to warm his bottle before giving it to him."

Shaking his head, he pulled his cell phone from the holster at his waist and offered it to her. "Call her. You aren't going to be able to relax until you do."

She eyed the phone a moment, then pushed his hand away. "No. Mary knows how to take care of a baby."

Chuckling, he slid the phone back into the holster. "Seems as if I've heard that before."

She made a face at him, then turned to peer out the passenger window, watching the scenery that swept past. "Where are we going?" she asked, after a moment.

"Austin. I thought I'd show you some of the sights." He glanced her way. "Have you ever seen the State Capitol?"

She shook her head. "No. In fact, I've never been to Austin, other than driving through, of course, but that doesn't count."

"I'll give you the five-dollar tour some other time. Today we'll just hit the high spots."

The high spots, it seemed, included a drive down Sixth Street, which, according to Mack, was Austin's version of New Orleans's Bourbon Street. From there, he drove her by the state capitol and shared with her the story of how some men full of Texas pride had schemed to construct a building, without breaking any laws, that would exceed the height of the U.S. Capitol in Washington, D.C., by choosing a hill as their building site. They enjoyed a relaxing stroll through Lady Bird Johnson's Wildflower Center, where Mack insisted on buying her a huge bag of bluebonnet seeds she stopped to admire. Then, late that afternoon, he rented a canoe on Town Lake, situated in the heart of downtown Austin, and gave her an entirely different perspective of the city, this time from the water.

The sun was just beginning its descent, turning the horizon blood red, when he pulled the oar from the water and rested it across his thighs, letting the canoe drift.

"A penny for your thoughts," he teased.

More relaxed than she'd been in what seemed like ages, Addy hid a smile as she leaned to trail her fingers through the water. "I'd take you up on that, if I had any."

Catching her hand, he set aside the oar and tugged her over to sit on his lap.

She gasped, clinging to his neck, as the canoe rocked precariously from side to side. "What are you trying to do?" she cried. "Drown us?"

Chuckling, he wrapped his arms around her waist. "No. Just wanted you closer."

She melted at his response and smiled, as she stroked his windswept hair back from his face. "You could've just asked, you know. What if I'd fallen in?"

Since his face was even with her breasts, he was unable to resist nipping at her nipple. "I'd have jumped in and saved you."

She sucked in a breath, then released it with a shiver. "Watch it, buster," she warned and pressed the tip of her finger against the center of his forehead to push him back. "There are laws against public groping."

"That wasn't groping." His gaze on hers, he slipped a hand beneath her dress and stroked his fingers up her thigh. "This is groping."

Even as his fingers molded her mound, he took her mouth with his, stealing her breath. The heat was instantaneous, bone melting.

"Mack," she begged, her breath hot against his lips. "You shouldn't. Someone might see."

He swung her legs around, bunching her dress up around her waist, until she was straddling him. "Who?" he challenged. "There's nobody out here but you and me."

She stole an uneasy glance around and discovered that he was right. They truly were alone. The canoe had drifted into a narrow inlet, darkened by the canopy of trees whose limbs draped overhead. In the far distance, lights gleamed from businesses that lined the opposite shoreline, but the area immediately around them was webbed with shadows of dusk, creating a private spot perfect for lovers.

He tugged on the string that crisscrossed her breasts, loosening it and pressed his lips in the valley he exposed.

"Ever made love in a canoe?" he asked, as he swept his tongue up her chest toward her chin.

She dropped her head back and closed her eyes. "N-no," she said breathlessly. "I don't think so."

He drew her hips up against his. "Good. Then this'll be a first for us both."

That night Addy lay with Mack spooned at her back, her head pillowed by one of his arms, the other hooked loosely over her waist. The fit was near perfect, the peace that filled her beyond anything she'd ever known, ever imagined.

She supposed she owed Ty a debt of gratitude—although she'd cut out her tongue before she'd ever tell him so. If not for Ty, she never would've met Mack.

Realizing how different her life would be without Mack a part of it, how empty, she linked her fingers with his, finding reassurance and comfort even in that slight connection.

So this is what it feels like to be in love, she thought with a shiver. She glanced over her shoulder to peer at the man responsible for her making the fall, and her heart turned to mush. He looked so boyish, with his hair all tousled and his face relaxed in sleep. So peaceful. Did he love her? she wondered uncertainly. He hadn't said the *L* word. But then, neither had she.

Setting her jaw, she turned her face away and settled her head on the pillow in front of his again. Don't get ahead of yourself, she lectured silently. It was like Mack had said earlier that day, when she'd asked if he was taking her on a date. They'd missed a few steps along the way. Virtual strangers, they'd married, become lovers. Now they would have to take the time to explore the possibilities, get to know each other, see where their feelings took them.

Gulping, she crossed her fingers and sent up a silent prayer that he would discover that he had fallen in love with her, too.

Johnny Mack let out a wail, and Addy flung back the covers, but Mack tightened his arm around her waist, stopping her before she could rise.

He pushed himself up to an elbow and pressed a sleepy kiss to the back of her neck. "Stay in bed. I'll check on him."

Though she was more awake than he, she lay back down and watched his shadowed form disappear into the nursery.

"Hey, little buddy," she heard him whisper to the baby. "What are you doing awake at this hour?"

Smiling, she closed her eyes, able to monitor his movements by the sounds coming from the nursery. The light metallic grate of the crib's guard rail being lowered. The wooden creak of the rocker accepting Mack's weight. The husky croon of Mack's voice as he soothed the baby. She grew sleepy, listening, as comforted by the sound of his voice as Johnny Mack seemed to be.

How lucky her son was to have Mack, she thought as sleep tugged her toward the brink. She'd never had a father to soothe her tears or rock her to sleep. But her son would always have Mack.

Seven

Mack sat before his lawyer's desk, listening carefully as Lenny explained the legal requirements of the request he'd made.

When Lenny was finished, Mack absorbed the information a moment, then said, "Let me see if I understand this correctly. You prepare the document necessary for Ty to forfeit all paternity rights and once he signs them, that's it? Johnny Mack is legally mine?"

"Legally he's already yours. The adoption papers we filed took care of that. Addy's refusal to name the father on the birth certificate simplified the process." He lifted his hands. "But since we both know Ty is the baby's biological father and are aware of his propensity to cause trouble for you, the forfeiture of paternity rights adds further protection should he ever choose to challenge the adoption."

"Then let's do it. I don't want Ty to have any legal claim on my son."

Lenny nodded. "All right. But I feel I should warn you. This is going to cost you, and I'm not talking about my legal fees. Ty will use this an opportunity to squeeze more money from you."

Mack stood and snugged on his hat, preparing to leave. "We'll worry about that if and when it happens. What we need to focus on now is locating Ty. Hire a private investigator. Ty usually leaves a trail of destruction a mile wide in his wake, so locating him shouldn't be too hard."

"Will do." Lenny rose and followed him to the door. "You didn't mention Addy. How are the two of you getting along?"

Mack ducked his head to hide a smile, nodded. "Good. Real good."

Lenny looked at Mack closely. "Well, I'll be damned," he murmured, then laughed and clapped Mack on the back. "Who'd have thought that an old coot like you would ever fall in love again?"

Zadie was gone four days, nine hours and twenty-two minutes. Addy knew, because she'd thoroughly enjoyed each and every second she'd spent in the kitchen during her absence. But that freedom was soon coming to an end, as Zadie was due to return that afternoon.

"You scrub that sink much more," Mary warned, "you're going to rub a hole in it."

With a sigh, Addy dropped the dishcloth in the sink, then glanced around the kitchen, looking for anything out of place. "It looks the same, doesn't it?" she asked uneasily. "I've put everything back just the way she had it."

"Would you quit worrying?" Mary fussed. "It's *your* kitchen, not Zadie's. You can paint the walls fire engine red, if you want. You don't need her permission."

"Yeah, right," Addy said dryly. "Zadie would hang me by my toes if I so much as moved the dust mop, without asking her first."

Mary wagged her head. "I can't believe you've let that woman bully you into believing she's the boss around here. *You're* the boss. Mr. Mack's wife. Remind her of that, and I'll bet she'll sing a different tune."

"You really think so?" Addy asked doubtfully.

"Wouldn't say it, if I didn't consider it the gospel truth."

"I don't want to make her mad. I really do like her." She wrinkled her nose. "It's just that she's so possessive about the kitchen."

"Stand up to her," Mary advised. "She's had the run of this place long enough."

Addy squared her shoulders. "All right. But you have to promise me one thing."

"What's that?"

"After they bury me, you have to paint the kitchen fire-engine red."

Mary blinked, then hooted a laugh. "Girl, you've got yourself a deal."

In spite of her brave talk, Addy made another sweep

through the kitchen, checking to make sure she'd returned everything to its proper place.

She was standing in the pantry, straightening the canned goods on the shelf, when she heard the back door open. Sure that it was Zadie returning, she was tempted to pull the door closed and hide. All but trembling in fear, she listened as Zadie shuffled into the kitchen and set down her overnight bag.

"Would you look at that," she heard Zadie mutter under her breath. "Somebody left the dishcloth in the sink to sour."

Addy winced, remembering too late that she'd failed to spread the dishcloth out over the drainboard to dry, as was Zadie's habit.

"Well, hi, Zadie," she heard Mary say, as the housekeeper entered the kitchen. "How's Mabel doing?"

"Good as can be expected, I guess."

"I'm surprised you didn't stay with her longer."

"Her daughter came from Tyler to see after her. Just as well. I 'bout worked myself to death cleanin' that house. I swear that woman lives like a pig. Had to scrub down the kitchen 'for I could even cook a meal."

As Mary passed by the pantry, she reached to close the door. When she saw Addy cowering inside, she pressed her lips together to smother a laugh and walked on, leaving the door open a crack.

"I 'magine Mr. Mack will be glad to see I'm home," Zadie said. "Poor man's probably half-starved by now."

Addy curled her nose in a snarl at the jab at her cooking abilities.

"Actually," Mary replied, quick to come to Addy's defense, "he's fit as a fiddle. Addy's cooked him three squares a day."

Addy beamed a smile. It quickly morphed to a scowl, when she heard Zadie's "humph."

Deciding it was high time she put Zadie in her place, she pushed open the pantry door and stepped out.

"Well, hello, Zadie," she said in surprise, as if she was unaware Zadie had returned and hadn't heard every word the woman had uttered since entering the house. "How's Mabel feeling?"

Zadie's eyes went round as saucers. "Uh—" she shot Mary a panicked look "—she's gettin' along real good. Real good."

Smiling sweetly, Addy braced a hip against the island and folded her arms across her chest. "I'm glad to hear that. Being waited on hand and foot gets old after a while."

"Yeah," Zadie agreed, and shot Mary another look. "I 'magine it do."

Addy looked around the room, considering. "You know," she said thoughtfully. "These walls could use freshening up."

Zadie swelled her chest in indignation. "Why, ain't nothin' wrong with these walls."

"Not the walls, per se," Addy conceded. "It's the color that needs sprucing."

"Ain't nothin' wrong with the color, either."

"But it's so…drab." She glanced at Mary, who was struggling not to laugh. "What do you think, Mary? Don't you think the walls need some color?"

"I like color," Mary agreed, playing along with Addy. "Brings life to a room."

Zadie looked as if she were about to explode. "This room's got enough life in it. Don't need no more."

"What color were you thinking of painting it, Addy?" Mary asked, egging her on.

Addy puckered her lips thoughtfully. "I don't know. Something strong. Vibrant. Maybe red."

"Red!" Zadie cried. "You ain't turnin' my kitchen into no whorehouse."

The back door opened and Mack strode in, stopped short. "Well, hi, Zadie," he said, in surprise. "I wasn't expecting you back so soon. Welcome home."

"Thank you, Mr. Mack," she replied, and shot Addy a frown. "Looks like I got back jist in the nick of time."

He tossed his hat onto the counter and looked at her curiously. "In time for what?"

Zadie tossed up her hands. "To save my kitchen, that's what. She's wantin' to paint it red."

Mack glanced at Addy. "Red?"

She smiled weakly. "Maybe not red. I just thought the kitchen could use some freshening up."

Mack glanced around the room, as if considering, then nodded. "You're right. It could stand to be repainted. Let me know when you decide on a color, and I'll hire a crew to come in and do the work." He glanced at his watch. "I need to make a couple of phone calls." He stopped in front of Addy and gave her a kiss full on the lips, then headed for the door. "If you ladies need me," he called over his shoulder, "I'll be in my office."

Zadie stood staring, her mouth open wide enough to catch flies, obviously shocked by the kiss she'd just witnessed.

Addy lifted a brow. "Problem?"

Zadie pursed her lips. "Well, I guess I don't need to be askin' who's sleepin' where," she muttered. "And here I was thinkin' I was gonna have to lock the two of you up in a room together, 'fore y'all figured out what a man and woman was created to do."

Addy pushed herself up to an elbow and swept her hair back from her face. "And then she said she was afraid she was going to have to lock us up in a room together so we could figure out what a woman and a man were created to do."

Chuckling, Mack stroked a hand along the curve of her waist. "She probably would've, too."

Addy snuggled close to his side, folding her hands between her head and his chest. "It's weird. Creepy even."

He drew back to look at her. "What?"

"Having someone living in the same house with us and her knowing what we're doing every second of the day, even where we're sleeping."

A laugh rumbled in his chest. "It's not as if we're doing something illegal."

She lifted her head to frown at him, then laid it back on his chest. "You know what I mean." She stifled a shudder. "It's creepy. Makes me feel like I'm on camera or something."

He stroked his fingertips lazily down her side. "Her

apartment is on the other end of the house," he reminded her. "She seldom comes to this wing of the house."

"Yeah, but still…"

Chuckling, he rolled to his side and gathered her into his arms. "Would it make you feel better if I had an apartment built for her separate from the house?"

She hid a smile, secretly pleased that he would go to such lengths just to make her happy. "No. But you might consider getting her ear plugs."

He lifted a brow. "You're a screamer?"

She drew a circle on his chest with a nail and shrugged. "If properly aroused."

"Since I've never heard you scream, am I supposed to take that as an insult?"

She gave him a coy look. "Or a challenge."

Laughing, he pulled her over on top of him and gripped her buttocks in his hands. "Nobody enjoys a challenge more than I do."

Smiling, she inched up his chest until her mouth was a breath away from his. "Lucky you. It just so happens I'm in the mood to scream."

"Found him in Houston," Lenny told Mack, then spun the file around on his desk for Mack to read. "He's shacked up with a woman in a condo near the Galleria. Been there about five months, best the P.I. can figure."

Mack studied the picture of the leggy blonde captured on film walking down the sidewalk, her arm linked through Ty's. "Looks like his type," he commented, then pushed the file back toward Lenny and sank into his chair. "Have you made contact with him?"

"This morning." Lenny shook his head sadly. "Ten o'clock in the morning and I woke him out of a dead sleep."

"I take it he's unemployed."

"Appears that way. The P.I. said when he leaves the condo, he has the woman in tow."

"Is she wealthy?"

"Lives off a trust fund set up by her grandfather. From her financials, if she's careful, she'll never have to work a day in her life."

Mack snorted. "A year, two at the latest, and Ty will drain her dry."

Lenny tipped his head in acknowledgment. "If his past spending habits are any indication, you're probably right."

"So, what have you got planned?"

Lenny pulled a file from the drawer on his left. "The document is prepared and ready for his signature. I've arranged for a notary public to meet you at the Houston airport at three o'clock tomorrow afternoon to witness Ty signing, and advised Ty of the same."

"He agreed to meet me?"

Lenny gave him a droll look. "What do you think? All I had to say was the word *paternity* and he was scrambling for a pen."

Mack shook his head. "He'll never grow up."

"Oh, he grew up, all right," Lenny said, then added dryly, "Too bad his brain didn't develop at the same rate."

* * *

Mack tossed his toiletry bag into his suitcase and crossed to the closet to pull out a shirt. "It's fairly cut-and-dried," he explained to Addy. "I give Ty the document Lenny prepared, he signs it, the notary stamps it with his seal, and we're done."

He stripped the shirt from the hanger, as he walked back to the bed. Addy took it from him and carefully folded it, her forehead pleated with worry.

"And that's the end of it?" she asked uncertainly, as she tucked the shirt into his suitcase. "He can never challenge his parental right to Johnny Mack?"

"Nope. Once he signs the document, he gives up all rights to our son."

Addy pressed a hand against her chest, touched by Mack's reference to Johnny Mack as their son, rather than just hers. Blinking back tears, she dropped her hand to reach for his and linked her fingers with his. "You'll be careful, won't you?"

His gaze on hers, he brought their joined hands to his lips and pressed a kiss against her knuckles. "Ty might be many things, but he's not violent. He won't hurt me."

Though she'd never seen any evidence of violence in Ty, she couldn't shake free from the premonition of doom that had shadowed her thoughts ever since Mack had returned from the lawyer's office and told her of his plans to go to Houston.

Forcing a smile, she gave his hand a squeeze and released it. "Just the same, be careful. I don't want anything happening to you."

"I'll be fine." He zipped his bag closed and hefted it from the bed.

It was all she could do to keep from throwing herself at his feet and begging him not to go.

"Do you really need to leave tonight?" she asked, trying to think of a way to delay his departure. "You're not scheduled to meet him until tomorrow afternoon."

"I don't want to take a chance on traffic or car trouble keeping me from getting to the airport by three."

"But you could leave early in the morning and make it to the airport with time to spare."

Shaking his head, he slung an arm around her shoulders and hugged her against his side, as he walked with her to the nursery door. "Would you stop worrying? I'm going to be fine."

She pressed her head against his shoulder as they entered the nursery, then eased from his embrace as he stopped before the crib and set his suitcase on the floor. Tears filled her eyes as he leaned over the crib and brushed his fingers over Johnny Mack's cheek.

"You be good while I'm gone," he whispered to the sleeping baby. "And take good care of your mommy for me." He bent over and pressed a kiss to Johnny Mack's forehead, then straightened and simply looked at him, a hand cupped at the top of the infant's head.

After a moment he picked up his suitcase and hooked an arm around Addy's waist. "If he wakes up in the night," he whispered as he guided her from the nursery, "try singing to him. He seems to favor country-western.

Two verses of a George Strait song usually puts him right back to sleep."

He stopped in the doorway of what she had come to think of as "their" room and placed a hand on her cheek. "Let's say our goodbyes here," he suggested quietly. "If I kiss you 'bye at the door, Zadie might expect one, too."

Laughing through the tears that filled her eyes, she wrapped her arms around his neck and hugged him tight. "Be safe," she whispered.

"You, too."

He kissed her, lingering a moment, then sealed it with another quick kiss and turned away. "See you tomorrow."

She lifted a hand as he walked away. When he reached the turn in the hallway that led to the front of the house, panic seized her. "Mack! Wait!"

He stopped, turned. "Yes?"

With tears blurring her vision, she pressed a hand to her lips to hold back the three words her heart screamed for her to say.

Dropping her hand to her side, she said instead, "Don't forget to put on your seatbelt."

The smile he offered her was soft, the look in his eyes warm. "I won't forget. 'Night, Addy."

He turned and rounded the corner, disappearing from sight.

"'Night, Mack," she whispered.

Mack offered his hand to the notary public seated at the table at the airport bar. "Mack McGruder," he said, by way of introduction.

The man stood, his grip firm as he shook Mack's hand. "Glen Powell."

Mack juggled the briefcase nervously in his hand, as he looked around. "Ty hasn't made it yet?"

Glen sat back down. "Not so far as I know." He glanced at his wrist watch. "It's not quite three, though. He's got some time."

Releasing a nervous breath, Mack propped the briefcase on a chair, then sat down opposite the notary public. A waitress appeared at his side and he ordered a beer, hoping it would calm his nerves. He hadn't slept much the night before, which is why he'd insisted on going to Houston a day early. He'd known if he'd stayed at home, he wouldn't have been able to hide his nervousness from Addy, and he didn't want his uneasiness to infect her. She was worried enough as it was.

Not that there was anything to worry about, he reminded himself. There was no reason to think that Ty would balk at signing the papers. He'd signed the other paternal releases Mack had presented him with without batting an eye.

The waitress arrived with Mack's beer and he gulped a swallow, then glanced toward the wide aisle beyond the bar's entrance, where passengers hustled past in both directions. hurrying to meet their flights. Not a sign of Ty, though.

He rolled his wrist, checked the time: 3:05. He set his jaw, refusing to accept Ty's tardiness as a sign his half brother wasn't going to show. Ty was always late, he reminded himself. Time meant nothing to a man who had nothing to do, nowhere to go.

* * *

Addy ran out the front door, clutching the baby in one arm and waving the other frantically over her head. "Zadie! Wait!"

Her lips pursed in disgust, Zadie cranked down her window. "What'd you forget this time?" she asked sourly.

"A bottle of champagne. Mack will be home tonight and we'll want to celebrate."

Rolling her eyes, Zadie cranked the window back up and drove away.

"Hag," Addy muttered under her breath, then nuzzled her nose against Johnny Mack's cheek. "She really loves us," she told him. "She just has a hard time showing her feelings."

He pumped his legs and arms as if trying to fly, and made Addy laugh. "You little doll," she said, hugging him to her, as she stepped back into the house. "How about a bath?" she asked him, as she headed back to her suite of rooms. "You can blow bubbles and splash all you want."

He pumped his legs again in excitement, as if he understood exactly what she was saying.

"You are way too smart," she informed him, as she set out the items needed for his bath on the bathroom vanity. Placing him on the elevated platform of his tub, she began removing his clothes. "Mack will be home tonight," she told him, then couldn't resist tickling him under his chin. "I'll bet he missed you. Did you miss him?"

He stared at her, his eyes round, listening intently.

She turned on the tap and waved her fingers beneath the stream of water, testing the temperature. "Mack's a good man," she went on. "You're lucky to have a father who loves you so much." Slipping the bath mitt over her hand, she squirted soap over her palm. "I never knew my father. Did you know that? He died before I was born."

She wrinkled her nose and leaned to bump it against the baby's. "Sad, huh? Not having a father?" Smiling, she began to rub the soapy mitt over his stomach. "But you'll always have Mack. He loves you so much. And he's a good father," she assured him, as she worked her way down his stomach to his legs. "Not many daddies would get up in the night like he does with you. Let's scrub your back," she said, and slipped a hand beneath him to lift him up far enough to soap his back side.

"There," she said, after rinsing him off. "All clean." Taking the hooded towel she'd laid out, she picked him up and wrapped it around him. "Ready for a diaper and some clean clothes?" she asked, continuing the one-sided conversation.

Entering the nursery, she balanced him in the crook of her arm, while plucking a romper from his chest of drawers. Cooing to him, she quickly diapered him and fumbled him into his clothes. "There," she said, at last. "All dressed for the day. How about if we rock while you nurse?" she asked as she sat down in the chair. Settling Johnny Mack in her arms, she opened her blouse and offered him her breast. A loving smile curved her lips, as he latched on to the nipple and began to suckle.

She pushed her foot against the floor to set the rocker into motion and began to hum. As he nursed, her mind drifted to the worries that had huddled on the edge of her mind since Mack had left the night before. Specifically Mack's meeting with Ty.

Closing her eyes, she laid her head back, silently praying that all would go well and Mack would return with Ty's signature on the document. With the tune of the George Strait song she hummed serving as background music, she let images of Mack sift through her mind. Mack standing beside her bed during Johnny Mack's birth, his hand gripped tightly around hers, his forehead creased in concentration, his blue eyes fixed on hers. Mack standing at her side in her hospital room, her arm looped through the crook of his, his hand folded over hers, as Pastor Nolan had pronounced them man and wife. Mack sitting in the rocking chair, his smile tender, his gaze on Johnny Mack as he rocked Johnny Mack to sleep. Mack asleep in her bed, his legs twined with hers, his arms around her, his breath warm on her cheek.

"Well, look who we have here."

She jumped, flipped open her eyes to find Ty standing in the doorway that opened to her bedroom. She gulped, instinctively tightening her arms around Johnny Mack. "Wh-what are you doing here?"

"I think that would be obvious." Smiling broadly, he opened his arms in an expansive gesture. "I came to see my family."

She turned a shoulder, as if to protect Johnny Mack from him. "Mack's not here."

"Addy, Addy," he scolded gently, as he stepped into the nursery. "I didn't come to see Mack. I came to see you. Our baby."

She curled herself further around her son. "He isn't yours."

Stopping in front of the rocker, he lifted a brow. "Do you really expect me to believe that baby is Mack's? Well, it's easy enough to do the math." He gestured to the baby. "He's, what? A month old? Let's see, the last time I saw you was in December, which was about five or six months ago, give or take a week. At the time, you claimed to be two months pregnant, and we'd been living together at least four months prior to that." His smile turned smug. "So, yes, the baby is definitely mine."

"He's not yours!" she cried. "He's Mack's. Mack adopted him."

"And why would Mack want to adopt a baby? A man his age? What would he hope to gain by taking on the responsibility of raising another man's child?"

When she only glared at him, he hunkered down in front of his chair. "You're no fool, Addy. Think. Mack's forty-two years old. A widower. He lost his wife and son in an automobile accident."

She swung her knees to the side, angling her body away from him. "No. I'm not listening to you."

"Oh, but you are," he replied calmly. "And your mind's working, isn't it? You're wondering why Mack would want the child of the half brother he openly admits he despises."

He laid a hand on her knee, and she knocked it away.

"Don't touch me! Don't you dare touch me ever again."

He shrugged and stood. "No skin off my back. You never were much fun in bed."

Repulsed by the sight of him, she turned her face away, refusing to look at him any longer. "Leave. Get out of this house or I'll call the police."

"Oh, I wouldn't do that, if I were you. Just think of all the gossip that would create. Everyone in town would know that I'm the baby's father, not Mack."

She glared at him, hate radiating from her eyes. "If it's money you want, I don't have any."

A slow smile spread across his face. "Mack does. Buckets of it. And I bet he'd pay a pretty price for my son. He thought he could get him for nothing. Have me sign the papers and give up my rights." He bent over, bracing his hands on his knees to put his face level with hers.

"That's why he went to Houston, wasn't it? To have me sign my rights away? He wanted my signature on the dotted line before I found out he wanted my kid for himself. But guess what, Addy? I'm smarter than my brother thinks. The P.I. he hired to find me was sloppy. I made him the first day he was on the job. I suspected Mack was the one who'd hired him. Then I get the call from Lenny, asking me to meet Mack to sign a paternity release, and my suspicions were confirmed.

"Call me paranoid, but something just didn't feel right about the whole setup. So I made a few calls to some old friends of mine in Lampasas. Imagine my surprise, when I learned that Mack had recently got married, and to a woman with a newborn, no less. A woman from Dallas. Since I'd left a pregnant woman in Dallas, it made me wonder. What I couldn't figure out was how the two of you got together.

"Then I remembered how anal Mack's always been about tying up loose ends, especially those that pertain to me. Considers it his God-given duty to protect the family name, his precious estate. So I put two and two together. Figured he'd somehow heard about you, knew you were pregnant and went to Dallas to buy you off." He lifted a brow in question. "Have I got the story right so far?"

She gulped, unable to tear her gaze from his, but refused to answer.

Straightening, he looked down at her and smiled. "No need to reply, Addy. I got the answer I wanted. You never could keep a poker face." He hunkered down again, holding his hand against the side of his mouth, as if about to share a secret. "Just between you and me, Addy," he said confidentially. "I don't give a rat's ass about the baby." He dropped his hand and grinned. "But Mack's going to pay for the right to call the kid his. I don't give away anything for free. Not even something I don't want."

Seething, Addy bared her teeth. "You have no right. You never wanted the baby. You ran so that you wouldn't have to accept responsibility for him."

He shrugged, unfazed by her accusations. "Why would I want the brat? But what you should be asking yourself is why *Mack* would want him. Do you suppose it's out of pity?" he asked curiously. "He felt sorry for the poor, defenseless unwed mother, left to raise a baby on her own, and decided to step in like the white knight he likes to think he is and save the day." He leaned a little closer. "Or maybe his reason was purely selfish. Mack needs an heir. His son is dead. He doesn't have anyone to leave all his money to, his estate."

"That's a lie," she cried angrily. "Mack isn't selfish. He's good and honest and generous."

Ty straightened to his full height and lifted a brow. "Oh, really? Has he ever mentioned how he feels about me?"

Addy gulped, remembering the things Mack had shared with her about his and his half brother's relationship. "Only that your relationship is…strained."

"Strained?" He tipped back his head and hooted a laugh. "Well, I guess that's one way of describing it. Mack hates me," he said bluntly. "Resented me from the day I was born, because our mother favored me over him."

She didn't believe him for a minute, but held her tongue, fearing that if she challenged his claim it would make him angry and he might do something rash.

"That's why he wanted to marry you and adopt my son," he went on. "Not because he's generous and kind. But because he'll do anything to keep me from getting a penny of what he considers his. Even marry a complete stranger and adopt her son. A son," he added, lifting a brow, "who shares some of the same blood that runs through Mack's veins."

Addy went as still as death. "Mack didn't adopt my baby because of any blood-tie. He loves Johnny Mack as if he were his own."

He snorted a laugh. "Don't kid yourself, Addy. Mack McGruder loves only one person. Himself."

"That's not true! He loves us."

"Us?" he repeated, then gave her a pitying look.

"Please tell me that you don't think Mack's in love with you just because he's slept with you? Hell, he's a man, Addy! One woman is the same as any other."

She felt tears burning behind her eyes and fought them back.

He shook his head in wonder. "Man, oh man. I've got to give my big brother credit for pulling off the perfect coup. He not only got himself an heir, he gets sex on demand."

He opened his hands. "But, hey. What does all this really matter? Whatever Mack's reasons for marrying you and adopting your brat, you're still the winner, right? You've landed yourself in high cotton." He spread his arms, indicating the house. "Not bad, huh? And quite a step up from that cracker box you were living in in Dallas. Of course, there's all his money, too. He's got tons of it socked away. But I'm sure you already know that."

He hunkered down in front of her again, bracing an arm on his thigh, and looked her square in the eye. "Now here's the deal, Addy. I want some of that money, too. A lot of it, in fact. And you're going to help me get it. If you do, you get to keep the brat and live a life of luxury as Mack's wife." He lifted a finger in warning. "But try cutting me out of the winnings, and I'll stake my claim on the baby and you'll be back in Dallas scrubbing out bed pans again."

"Git your hands up and your ass out of Mr. Mack's house."

Addy snapped up her head to find Zadie standing in

the doorway, the stock of Mack's rifle braced against her shoulder, the barrel aimed at Ty's back.

Ty stood. "Now, Zadie," he scolded in a voice that all but dripped sugar. "You know as well as I do that you'd never shoot me. Hell, you helped raise me."

She flipped off the safety, but kept the barrel aimed at Ty's chest. "Should'a drowned you when you was a baby and saved us all the shame you brung to this family."

"Now, Zadie," he began, and took a step toward her.

The metallic click of the rifle being cocked silenced him and had him throwing up his hands.

"Don't think for a minute I won't pull this trigger," she warned. "Now, git outta this house. And don't think 'bout coming back and terrorizing this family anymore. If you do, I'll fill your heart with lead."

Ty obviously believed her, because he skirted a wide path around Zadie, as he made his way to the door, his hands high over his head. Zadie followed at a safe distance, keeping the rifle aimed at his back.

Trembling, Addy sank back in the rocking chair, her arms locked around Johnny Mack. She was still sitting there when Zadie returned a few moments later, the rifle now at her side, its barrel pointed at the floor.

"You okay, Miss Addy?" she asked hesitantly.

Addy drew what felt like the first real breath she'd drawn since she'd looked up and found Ty standing in the doorway. "Y-yes. He didn't hurt me."

"And won't. He's gone now. I made sure of that, and locked the doors up tight when I came back inside."

Numb, Addy nodded. "Thank you, Zadie."

Frowning, Zadie propped the rifle against the door. "Why'd you let that no-count boy in this house, in the first place?" she fussed. "You shoulda knowed he was up to no good."

Addy shook her head. "I didn't let him in. He just… appeared."

Zadie's frown deepened. "Must have sneaked through the gates when I left for the grocery store." Shaking her head, she crossed to Addy. "Here, honey. Give me that baby. You're shakin' like a leaf."

Addy tightened her arms around Johnny Mack. "No."

Zadie planted her hands on her hips. "Well, you can't jist sit in that rocker all day and hold him."

When Addy refused to relinquish her hold on Johnny Mack, Zadie heaved a sigh of defeat. "All right, honey. You go on and rock that baby all you want. I 'magine your nerves are near shot. I know mine are." She forced a smile. "I know what we need. A good cup of strong tea. And I'll toss in a shot of whiskey. Just for medicinal purposes, mind you." She turned for the door. "You just sit right there and collect yourself. I'll bring the tea in here, once I've brewed it."

After Zadie left, Addy remained in the rocker, her body stiff, her eyes unblinking. She was numb, paralyzed, unable to move or think. Thoughts whirled through her mind too fast for her to grasp, while others seemed to scream obscenely for her attention.

He was lying, she told herself, fighting the doubts Ty had planted in her mind. Mack wasn't a mean person or a selfish one, as Ty had claimed. Mack was loving and giving. And he hadn't adopted Johnny Mack simply to get an heir. Mack genuinely loved Johnny Mack. Nothing Ty could say would ever convince her differently.

Sure, he loves the baby. But does he love you? Or does he just want sex from you, as Ty had claimed?

She gulped, unsure of the answer. Mack had never told her that he loved her. Not in so many words. He was kind to her, unbelievably generous, and the most extraordinary lover. But did he *love* her? As much as she loved him?

Tears filled her eyes. Oh, God, how she wanted him to. She wanted family so badly, yearned for what she had never known, been denied throughout her life. She thought she'd found that with Mack, had begun to believe that they could create a family. Not in the sense that she wanted it. She needed his love, his heart. She'd already lost hers to him and would accept nothing less in return, not even the semblance of family he'd offered to her when he'd married her.

Time, she reminded herself stubbornly. She and Mack were still feeling their way, just beginning to get to know each other. She knew he card for her. In time he would grow to love her as much as she loved him.

But what if they ran out of time?

Fear gripped her chest at the thought, its icy fingers winding their way up to her throat and squeezing. What if they ran out of time? What if Ty made good his threat? He'd claimed that if she didn't help him get money from Mack, he'd take her baby. She couldn't bear to lose her son. Nor could she bear the thought of Mack losing him.

And that's what frightened her most, she realized, at

last able to single out the true source of her fear. She was afraid that Ty would succeed in taking Johnny Mack away from Mack.

She had to do something to stop him, she told herself, her fear giving way to anger. She wouldn't be a part of Ty's scheme to blackmail Mack. She would never do anything to purposely hurt Mack.

But if she didn't do as Ty had told her, he would drag them all through an ugly court battle, suing for custody of a child he'd openly admitted he didn't want.

She gulped, barely able to swallow past the fear that rose to crowd her throat again. Without Ty's signature on the paternity release Lenny had prepared, he still possessed the rights accorded any natural father, rights that would supersede any that Mack was awarded when he'd adopted Johnny Mack. It was in the news all the time. Judges ruling in favor of a natural parent's right to a child and taking the child away from its adoptive parents.

She shot up from the rocker. She had to leave, she thought, her heart hammering wildly in her chest. With her gone, she would render Ty powerless, taking away the one bargaining chip he thought he had. Fool that he was, he thought she was as greedy as he, that she would be willing to do anything in order to live the life of luxury afforded her as Mack's wife. But he was wrong. Mack meant more to her than money. She would willingly sacrifice anything for his happiness and that of her son.

* * *

By the time Zadie returned with the promised cup of tea, Johnny Mack was bundled up in his car seat in the center of Addy's bed and Addy was packing.

Zadie froze in the doorway. "What are you doin'?" she cried in dismay.

Addy stuffed a stack of clothing into the suitcase. "I'm leaving."

Zadie's eyes shot wide. "What you mean, you's leaving?"

Addy crossed back to the dresser and scooped another stack of clothing from the drawer. "I'm going home. To Dallas."

Zadie bustled into the room and set the tea tray onto the top of the dresser. "Dallas ain't your home. This here is where you live now. Right here with Mr. Mack. What's he gonna think when he comes home and finds you gone? What's I supposed to tell him?"

Addy dumped the clothing into the suitcase and slammed the lid, locking it into place, then turned to face Zadie with a calm that would surprise her later.

"You can tell him to file for the annulment he promised me."

Eight

Fury burned through Mack's blood as he braked his car to a tire-squealing stop in front of his house. What a colossal waste of time, he thought angrily and shoved the gearshift into Park. And it was just like Ty to pull a stunt like this. Agreeing to a meeting, then not showing up. Wasting people's time. It was so like his half brother, Mack was amazed he hadn't expected it from the beginning.

With a weary sigh, he dropped his forehead to rest against the steering wheel. The hell of it was, now he had to go in and face Addy, tell her that he'd failed, that he'd come home empty-handed. She was going to be upset. Hell, *he* was upset! And she'd worry. No more than he would, but he'd hoped he could put to rest once and for all her fears that Ty would somehow cause trouble for them.

Heaving another sigh, he shouldered open the car door and climbed out. He paused a moment to stretch his arms above his head, straightening out the kinks sitting all day had put in his back, then dropped them to his sides and headed for the house.

He opened the door and stepped inside, closing it behind him. "Anybody home?" he called.

Zadie rushed from the kitchen and met him in the hallway, wringing her hands. "Oh, Mr. Mack," she said tearfully. "They's gone. Packed up and left."

His gut tightened in dread. "Addy's gone?"

"Yessir. Soon as Ty left, she packed up and lit out."

His heart seemed to stop. "Ty? He was here?"

"Yessir. When I left this mornin' to do the grocery shoppin', he must'a sneaked through the gate while it was still open. I didn't see him, but he was here at the house when I came back to get the grocery list I left sittin' on the kitchen counter." She pulled her apron up and buried her face in it. "It's all my fault," she wailed. "I shoulda never left her here by herself. I shoulda knowed that boy would do somethin' bad."

He grabbed her arms and gave her a shake. "He hurt her?"

She wiped her face on the apron and shook her head. "Not so you could see. But he musta said somethin' to make her run like she did."

"Where did she go?"

"Dallas. Said she was goin' home. I tried to make her

wait till you got back, but she wouldn't listen to nothin'
I said. Talkin' crazy, she was. Said for me to tell you to
file for that annulment you promised her."

Mack dropped his arms to his side. "No," he whispered, then spun away and dug his fists against his eyes.
"Oh God, please, no."

Mack wasn't about to lose Addy. He was going to
Dallas and he was bringing her and the baby back home
with him where they belonged.

But before he could do that, he had to settle some
business with Ty.

He didn't know what Ty had said to Addy, and really
didn't care. What he *did* know was that Ty was the one
who was responsible for her leaving, and Mack was
going to make damn sure that his half brother never had
the power to interfere in his life again.

Since his last attempt to meet with Ty had failed miserably, he decided to try a different tactic this time
around.

At 9:00 a.m. sharp, two days after Addy's departure,
he pulled into the parking lot of the condo in Houston
where Ty was currently living and gathered the bulky
file the P.I. had prepared for him under his arm, along
with the thinner and neater file of documents Lenny had
prepared, and climbed from his car. He shot a glance at
the car that pulled into the slot next to his, then headed
up the walk toward the condo.

Hoping that his half brother was true to form, he
leaned on the doorbell. He could hear the continuous

musical peel through the wooden door and smiled, knowing there was no way Ty could ignore the irritating sound for very long.

Within minutes, he heard the angry stomp of footsteps approaching from the other side of the door, and his half brother's muttered curses. He quickly stepped out of view, so that Ty couldn't see him through the peep hole, and waited.

The door was yanked open and Ty stepped out, wearing nothing but a pair of silk pajama pants and a scowl.

Mack pulled his finger from the doorbell. "Good morning, Ty."

"Go to hell," Ty growled and gave the door an angry shove.

Mack stuck his boot in the opening, before the door could slam in his face, and stepped inside.

"Nice place," he commented as he looked around.

Ty whirled, his face flushed an angry red. "What the hell do you want?"

Calmly Mack drew the folders from beneath his arm. "Since you missed our previous appointment, I thought I'd save us both the frustration of attempting to schedule another by dropping by unannounced."

"If that's a paternity release you've got, you're wasting your time. I'm not signing it."

"You might want to reconsider that decision," Mack suggested mildly.

Ty folded his arms across his bare chest, his stance cocky. "If you think you can waltz in here and bulldoze me into signing away my rights to the kid, you're wrong.

I'm a step ahead of you, big brother. I figured out your little scheme. That baby's mine and you're going to pay dearly to have it."

Unfazed, Mack flipped open the file folder Lenny had prepared for him. "Speaking of money, I have some financial statements that might interest you."

Ty eyed him suspiciously. "What financial statements?"

Ignoring the question, Mack peered around him. "Is there a place where we can sit down and discuss this more comfortably?"

Ty hesitated a moment, then dropped his arms with a sigh and turned away. "In here," he said and led the way into a living area that opened off the entry.

He gestured to a chair opposite the sofa. "Make it quick," he told Mack, before sprawling on the sofa. "I want to get back to bed."

Mack perched on the edge of the chair and opened Lenny's file on the coffee table in front of him. He picked up the first set of clipped documents and tossed them onto the coffee table in front of Ty.

"As you can see," he said, tipping his head to indicate the papers. "That is the Year-to-Date statement of the trust Mom set up for you, prior to her death."

Ty didn't so much as glance at the document. "So? I get one from the accountant every quarter."

"Do you ever read it?" Mack asked.

Ty shifted uncomfortably. "What's the use? It's just a bunch of numbers."

Mack leaned over and picked up the document. "If you'd bothered to read the report," he said as he flipped to the last page, "you'd know that the balance of your trust is zero, and has been for almost two years."

He had the satisfaction of watching Ty pale.

"That can't be right," Ty blustered. "Funds are deposited to my personal account every month, same as always."

Mack sank back in his chair. "Yes," he agreed. "But the funds haven't been coming from your trust. As I mentioned, that account bottomed out almost two years ago."

Ty shot to his feet. "That's bull!" he cried. "There was a million and a half in that trust."

Mack nodded. "And you managed to blow it all in a little over twelve years."

Ty dragged a hand over his hair, shooting it into spikes, as he paced away. "No way. There's no way in hell I spent all that money."

"Oh, but you did. And then some."

Ty whirled. "But I'm still getting money every month. I must have investments left that are paying dividends."

Mack shook his head. "You don't have any assets left. If you'll remember, you had the accountant turn all your assets into cash on your thirtieth birthday. Against my advice, I might add. As I recall, you wanted the cash to purchase a boat of some kind. A small yacht, wasn't it?"

Mack could see that his half brother was beginning to sweat, and knew he had him where he wanted him.

He dismissed the boat with a wave of his hand. "But that's old history," he said. "Out of respect to our mother," he went on, "I continued to make deposits to your account, using my own personal funds, to support you."

Wanting to give Ty a moment to absorb that information, before hitting him with the final blow, he leaned forward and picked up the statement. After placing it carefully back in the file, he sank back in the chair again and met Ty's gaze. "But I won't be making those deposits in the future."

The blood drained from Ty's face. "But how am I supposed to live? How will I pay my bills?"

Mack shrugged. "I suppose you could sell your yacht. That ought to be enough to keep you going until you can find employment."

Ty sagged down on the sofa with a groan and dropped his face into his hands.

It was all Mack could do to appear concerned. "Is there a problem?"

"The yacht's gone," Ty mumbled.

"Gone?" Mack repeated in confusion, though he'd already known Ty was no longer in possession of the yacht. The coastguard had confiscated it during a drug raid over a year ago, a bit of information the P.I. Mack had hired had discovered.

Ty dropped his hands and fell back against the sofa with a weary sigh. "Yeah, gone," he said miserably. "I loaned it to a buddy of mine, and he...well, he got into a little bit of trouble on his return from Mexico and the feds ended up with it."

Mack shook his head sadly. "That's a shame, Ty. A real shame." He glanced around the room, noting the expensive furniture and accessories. "Maybe the woman you're living with would be willing to support you, until you can find a job. Looks as if she could afford to."

Ty dropped his head back and dragged his hands down his face. "Not for long. She's already harping about me chipping in more."

"Well, gee," Mack said sympathetically, "that kind of puts you between a rock and a hard place, doesn't it?"

Ty lowered his chin to narrow an eye at Mack. "You knew all along, didn't you? All this talk about my finances was a set up, so you can get the kid."

Mack reached again for the file Lenny had prepared. "I'd rather think of it as laying all the cards on the table. Sounds much more civil, don't you think?"

He drew the second set of clipped pages from the file and tossed them onto the coffee table in front of Ty. "Those are the papers you were supposed to sign yesterday at the airport. To save you the time of fighting your way through all the legalese, it is a legal document Lenny prepared in which you forfeit all paternal rights to Addy's baby." A slow smile spread across his face. "But I guess you probably know what a Forfeiture of Paternity Rights consists of. You've signed enough of them over the years to know the verbiage by heart."

Scowling, Ty sat up and dragged the document closer. "So what do I get out of this?" he asked as he scanned it. "I deserve something out of this deal. I am the kid's father, after all."

"A responsibility you ran from," Mack reminded him.

Ty lifted his head and grinned. "Your gain, though, right? Come on, Mack, let's cut to the chase. How much is the kid worth to you?"

The world. But Mack wasn't about to let Ty know how much he loved Johnny Mack.

"You can't put a value on human life," he informed Ty wryly. He pulled the last set of clipped pages from the file, tossed them on top of the papers of forfeiture, then sank back in his chair and templed his fingers before his chest. "But I do feel a moral obligation to our mother. Before she died, she made me promise that I would look after you, a promise that I've honored for fourteen years. But I'm done, Ty. I won't be depositing any more money into your account, and I won't be bailing you out of trouble any longer. Your life is yours to live, and you'll have to deal with the consequences of how you choose to live it all on your own. I refuse to serve as your safety net any more."

He dipped his chin, indicating the last document he'd tossed to Ty. "I'm sure Lenny found a much more complicated way in which to state it, but that's pretty much what that document says. Your signature on the last page will acknowledge your understanding of what I've just explained to you. The same is needed on the Parental Forfeiture document, which will relieve you of any financial support required by the state and its courts now and any time in the future."

Ty quickly flipped to the last page, where a thin black line awaited his signature. "And if I don't sign?" he asked.

"As far as the document that spells out my financial responsibility to you in the future is concerned, it doesn't matter one way or the other. You've spent your trust, and what money I have is mine to spend as I see fit and I no longer feel an obligation to give any of it to you.

"But the document concerning your parental rights is a different matter. If you insist upon retaining your parental rights, then you will also be responsible for the child's support, which will be decided by a judge."

Ty snorted. "Hard to get blood out of a turnip. A judge can't order me to turn over money I don't have."

Mack flapped a hand, indicating the document Ty still held. "If you'll look at paragraph three on page one, you'll find that you do have some money. Not much, considering the amount you've blown, but enough to clear my conscience and give you the time you'll need to find yourself a job."

Ty quickly flipped back to the first page and scanned until he found paragraph three. "A hundred thousand dollars," he read in disbelief, then lifted his gaze to Mack's. "You're giving me a hundred thousand dollars?"

"If you'll read a little further, you'll discover that the gift is contingent on you signing the document."

Ty glanced down at the paper again. After a moment, he choked a laugh. "Oh, I get it now. This is a trick. A smooth one, I have to admit, but a trick nonetheless. If I sign this, but refuse to sign away my paternal rights, then I'm setting myself up to be stripped clean by some judge, who'll garnish a healthy portion of the funds as support for the kid."

Mack plucked a pen from the pocket of his shirt and tossed it onto the table. "In the eyes of the court, a child is entitled to support from his father."

Shaking his head, Ty picked up the pen.

"Wait just a second," Mack said, stopping him before he could sign his name. He rose and headed toward the front door.

"Where are you going?" Ty asked in frustration. "Let's get this over with."

"I intend to," Mack replied, then opened the door and waved a hand, signaling the men parked in the car beside his to come inside.

Ty stared, slack-jawed, as Mack's lawyer, preacher, banker, and childhood friend, Bill Johnson, followed him back into the room.

"Just to make everything legal," he explained to Ty, as he took his seat opposite his half brother again, then smiled. "I don't like leaving any loose ends."

"It's not that we're destitute," Addy assured Johnny Mack, as she cranked the handle of the infant swing she'd placed him in. "But having a little nest egg to fall back on for those little emergencies that tend to crop up certainly wouldn't hurt."

She set the swing in motion, then approached the trunk, dragging her sweaty palms across her rear end to dry them.

"Cross your fingers," she said to the baby and lifted the lid. Sinking to her knees, she began to pull out items.

"Good heavens," she fussed. "Would you look at all this junk?" Curling her nose in disgust, she pulled a dried corsage from inside, its flattened flowers yellow and brittle with age. "Why on earth did Mom save all this stuff?"

After ten minutes spent sorting and discarding without finding anything that closely resembled the torn piece of paper that had supposedly belonged to her father, Addy grew discouraged.

"I don't know why I'm wasting my time," she told the baby crossly as she pawed through the scattered items remaining on the bottom of the trunk. "If he really did send it to Mom, she would've thrown it away."

She froze when she caught a glimpse of an air mail envelope, its red and blue markings faded with time, but distinctive enough to recognize. Her fingers trembling, she pulled it from the trunk and sat down on the floor.

"It's stamped 'Vietnam,'" she told Johnny Mack, as she smoothed a hand over the front of the envelope. "But there's no name on the return address. Just an APO." She closed her eyes, promising herself she wouldn't be disappointed by whatever she found inside.

Bracing herself, she flipped up the flap and pulled out the letter enclosed. She said a quick prayer, then opened the folds. As she did, a piece of paper fell out. Her heart seemed to stop, as she watched it float to her lap.

"Johnny Mack," she whispered, as if the sound of her voice might cause the piece of paper to disintegrate if she spoke too loudly. "I found it. Oh, my God, I really found it!"

With her heart beating wildly in her chest, she lifted the scrap of paper to examine it. She frowned as she scanned the handwritten words, unable to make heads or tails of their meaning from the fragmented words. She quickly turned the paper over and looked at the back side. There she found a notary public's seal, a woman's name and what must be Antonio Rocci's signature.

She traced the tip of her finger along the scrawled letters of his name, awed that the signature was obviously written by her father's hand. "It's like touching him," she said to Johnny Mack, then gulped back the emotion that crowded her throat. "I never knew him, never saw him. He died before I was born."

She glanced up at her son, his image blurred by her tears. "He was your grandfather. Antonio Rocci was my father and your grandfather. This is his signature."

Johnny Mack kicked his feet and cooed, making the swing dance. Wanting, needing to share this moment with her son, Addy gathered the letter up and moved to sit in front of the swing.

"Let's see what the letter says," she told him and opened it to read aloud.

Dear Mary Claire,
You don't know me, so I feel I should introduce myself. My name is Larry Blair and I served alongside Tony in Vietnam. I was with him the day he died.

She lifted her head to peer wide-eyed at Johnny Mack. "The letter's not from him," she told Johnny Mack, then gulped and dropped her gaze to read on.

I know that what I'm about to tell you will in no way make up for the loss you have suffered, but I feel a tremendous burden to share my impressions of Tony with you.

I first met Tony in Austin the day we shipped out for San Francisco, the first leg in our journey to Vietnam. I didn't know his real name at the time, as the guys who'd attended boot camp with him had given him the nickname "Romeo." I guess it isn't much of a stretch for you to understand why they'd tag him as such. His Italian good looks and those dark eyes of his were hard for any woman to resist.

But Tony was a lot more than a pretty face. He had a heart as big as the state he called home and the kind of personality that made him a favorite with all the guys. Here in Vietnam, there are times when it's hard to find anything to laugh about. But when morale was low and everybody was suffering a bad case of the blues, we could always count on Tony to do or say something to pull us out of the muck.

He was a good friend to the guys he served with. One in particular, Preacher, Tony treated like a kid brother. He'd argue and fight with him some, kind of like brothers do, I guess. But when push came to shove, Tony was first in line to defend Preacher. Some of the men give Preacher a hard time because he is—well, I guess you'd say he is tender-hearted. The thought of shooting another human being, enemy or not, is something he can't bring himself to do. But Tony didn't hold that against Preacher the way the others did. In fact, he bloodied the noses of a few who dared call Preacher a coward.

As I said before, I was with Tony the day he was killed. The mission we were on was supposed to be "safe," but I guess there's no such thing in times of war. I won't go into the details of the battle, but I do want to tell you this. Tony was a brave soldier and gave his life to protect the men he served with.

The night before he was killed, Tony told me about the baby you carry. His baby. He said that he felt bad about running off and leaving you alone to take care of everything and wanted to do something to make things right. His plan was to send you a portion of his check each month. When he returned home, he hoped to find a job that paid more than a soldier's pay and be able to send you a larger sum for child support. I guess it goes without saying that he won't be able to do that now.

He made me promise him something that night, while we were talking. He made me promise that I would send you the piece of paper I've enclosed. Maybe I had better explain how he came to have this piece of paper. The night before we left for Vietnam, we were in a bar in Austin having a few drinks. We met a man there who had lost a son in the war. Since he no longer had anyone to leave his ranch to, he said he wanted to give it to us. He wrote out a bill of sale and tore it into pieces, giving each one a piece, then had a notary public witness each of our signatures.

I don't know if this will ever be worth anything, but Tony said he had nothing of any value to leave you, if something should happen to him, and wanted me to send you this.

I had hoped that I'd never have to fulfill my promise to him, and it grieves me that I have to now. I found your address among Tony's personal effects, and I'll hang on to it. I'll contact you after I get home and tell you what you need to do in order to get Tony's share of the ranch. Like I said before, there's no guarantees, but for Tony's sake, and that of his child, I hope this piece of paper turns out to be the inheritance he would've wanted his child to have.

Sincerely,

Sgt. Larry Blair

With tears streaming down her face, Addy stared at the letter, a hand pressed over the ache in her heart.

"Do you think this means he loved me?" Swiping a hand over her cheek, she lifted her head to look at the baby. "I mean, think about it. He told this Larry person he felt bad about leaving Mom to raise me alone and wanted to help support me. Even asked him to send Mom the piece of paper, in case he was killed, because it was all he had to give me."

Johnny Mack's lower lip quivered and he let out a wail.

Addy jumped up, stuffing the paper and envelope into the pocket of her robe. "Oh, baby, don't cry," she soothed, as she pulled him from the swing. "Just because Mommy's sad, doesn't mean you have to be sad, too." She tucked his head in the curve of her neck and pressed a kiss to his forehead. "You've got a daddy," she told him. "There's no need for you to cry. You've got Mack, and you'll always know that he loves you."

Mack parked his car in front of Addy's, then sat there for a minute, studying her house. The front windows were dark, but there was a light on in the rear of the house. It was late, probably too late to be making a social call, but he hadn't come this far to turn back now.

Drawing in a deep breath to steady his nerves, he climbed from his car and smoothed a hand over his hair, as he strode up the walk, knowing he probably looked like something the cat dragged in, after driving all day, first to Houston, then to Dallas. But he hadn't wanted to stop and shower and clean up. He'd wanted only to see Addy. He rapped his knuckles twice on the door, then waited. Unlike the last time he'd knocked on Addy's front door, her response was almost immediate. The porch light blinked on, nearly blinding him, and he heard her uneasy call of "Who's there?" from the other side of the thick wooden door.

"It's Mack. I need to talk to you."

A long stretch of silence followed his pronouncement, making him doubt his chances of getting inside. But then the door opened a crack, revealing a narrow slice of her face.

"Mack? Why are you here? It's late."

"I know and I'm sorry, but we need to talk."

She hesitated a moment, then asked, "About what?"

He bit down on his frustration. "Addy, would you please just let me in."

Though he could tell she'd rather not, she opened the door wider.

Relieved, he stepped inside and closed the door behind him. When he turned, he saw that her feet were bare and she wore a robe cinched at the waist. He glanced at his wristwatch and bit back a groan when he saw that it was past midnight. "I woke you," he said with real regret.

She eased back, as if wanting to keep a safe distance from him, and shook her head. "I wasn't asleep."

Biting down on his frustration, he glanced around. "Is there somewhere we can sit down? It's been a long day."

She hesitated a moment, then gestured to a doorway at her left. "In here." She led the way into the living room that opened off the entry, paused to switch on a lamp, then sat down in the chair opposite the sofa.

Willing to honor her need for distance—for the moment, anyway—he seated himself on the sofa.

"Did Zadie give you my message?"

He lifted a brow. "About the annulment?"

"Yes."

"Yeah. She told me."

"Have you notified Lenny?"

"Didn't see the point."

Her jaw sagged. "But you promised! You said if I ever wanted to end our agreement, you'd grant me an annulment."

"Annulment is no longer an option," he informed her. "If you'll remember, we consummated our marriage. An act that was your idea, if I recall."

She dropped her gaze, her cheeks reddening.

He wondered if she was remembering the night she seduced him. He did. Every detail. From the damp towel she'd dropped to the floor to the exquisite feel of her tight warmth surrounding him to the peace and contentment of having her body curled against his, as they'd slept.

"Why did you leave, Addy?" he asked quietly.

She snapped up her head, her eyes wide with surprise, then dropped her gaze to her lap again and began nervously pleating the ends of the sash that cinched her robe. "I…I thought it would be best."

"For who? You? The baby? It sure as hell wasn't for me."

She caught her lip between her teeth, but kept her head down. "F-for everyone."

"Come on, Addy," he chided. "I deserve more of an explanation than that."

She whipped up her head, her eyes filled with anger.

"What is it you want from me?" she cried. "You got the heir you wanted. That's why you married me."

He wanted to deny her claim, but to do so would be a lie. He had wanted an heir, had offered her marriage, in order to get one.

"That's true," he admitted. "Or at least it was in the beginning. But things changed. *I* changed."

Desperate to convince her, he slid from the sofa and knelt at her feet, closing a hand over those she gripped so tightly on her lap. "You were happy living with me, weren't you?"

She squeezed her eyes shut and turned her face away. "Mack, please," she begged. "Don't do this."

The tears in her eyes, her inability to answer his question proved to him that she loved him.

"Addy, look at me." When she stubbornly kept her face turned away, he cupped a hand at her cheek and forced her to face him. "Addy," he ordered gently. "Look at me and tell me that you weren't happy with me."

She flipped open her eyes. "Yes, I was happy with you!" she cried, tears now streaming down her face. "I fell in love with you! That's why I left. I couldn't let him hurt you, and if I'd stayed, he would."

He peered at her in confusion. "You mean Ty? Addy, Ty can't hurt me."

"He could've if I'd stayed!" She swept an angry hand across her wet cheeks. "He was going to use Johnny Mack as bait to extort money from you. He said that if I didn't help him get what he wanted, he would claim

Johnny Mack and I'd be back in Dallas scrubbing bed pans again."

He blinked, unable to make the leap from extortion to bed pans. "But how did you think your leaving was going to protect me from him?"

"Don't you see?" she cried in frustration. "It isn't Johnny Mack Ty wants, it's your money! If I'd stayed, Ty would have taken you to court and proven his paternity and you would've lost everything you've worked so hard for. By leaving and ending our marriage, I take you out of the picture and there's only me for him to deal with. Once he realizes the only thing he can gain out of a child custody battle with me is a child, he'll back off quick enough.

"And if he did try to fight me for custody, he'd lose. No judge in his right mind would turn a child over to a loser like Ty. Either way, I'll have full custody of Johnny Mack, and you can see him as often as you want. I know how much you love him, and he loves you. You're his *father*, Mack. I'd never try to keep the two of you apart."

Though he didn't understand her logic and found it impossible to follow, he wasn't about to question her further. She'd told him all he needed to know to convince him that she still loved him.

His smile tender, he cupped a hand at her cheek. "Oh, Addy. Though I appreciate the sacrifice you were willing to make, it isn't necessary. Ty can't hurt us. Not you, or me, or Johnny Mack. I've seen to that."

She went as still as death. "But...how?"

"He signed the papers."

She shook her head, refusing to believe him. "No. That's impossible. He was at the house with me when he was supposed to be meeting you in Houston."

"That's true, though I didn't know why he didn't show up until later. When I returned home and found you gone, I figured he had something to do with your leaving. I wanted more than anything to leave right then and there and come after you, bring you and the baby back home, but I knew I couldn't do it until I'd settled things with Ty once and for all. I spent yesterday getting all the legal documents ready that would sever my relationship with him, then drove to Houston this morning and had him sign them."

Eyes wide, she stared, as if afraid to believe what he was telling her was true. "And that's enough? His signature, I mean. That makes it all legal? He can't ever challenge the documents' validity?"

Mack snorted a laugh. "I'd like to see him try, considering he'd be questioning the integrity of the men I brought along to witness his signature."

She gulped, swallowed. "I…I don't know what to say," she said helplessly. "What to do."

He shifted to gather her face between his hands. "I do," he assured her. "Remember earlier when you asked me what more I wanted from you?"

She gulped again, nodded.

He swept a thumb beneath her lashes, catching a tear that shimmered there. "You, Addy. Only you. I love you more than life itself."

She closed her hands over his, going all but limp with relief. "Oh, Mack. I didn't know. You never said."

He looked at her curiously. "That I love you?"

She sniffed, nodded.

"Well, shame on me, then, although I'd swear I had."

She shook her head. "No. I'd remember something as important as that."

Chuckling, he bussed her a quick kiss. "Yeah, I'd imagine you would." He frowned thoughtfully, then shook his head. "I don't recall the exact moment I realized I'd fallen in love with you. It was before the night you seduced me, that much I know for sure. But I can't put my finger on exactly when, as it kind of slipped up on me, unexpected like. Kind of like the way we met. Unexpected, I mean. Seems we've done everything bass-akwards. Having a baby. Getting married. Falling in love."

He hauled in a breath. Released it, wanting to do this right. "When I proposed to you before, I offered you a marriage of convenience. I'd like to propose again, but this time I want the whole ball of wax. I want us to be husband and wife, in every sense of the word. I want us to be a real family."

"Oh, Mack," she whispered tearfully.

"Wait a minute," he said and stood, catching her hand to draw her to her feet, as well. "I nearly forgot something."

He stuffed his hand into his pocket and fished around for the ring he'd taken from the safe in his office before he'd left home that morning. Finding it, he took her left hand and placed the ring at the tip of her finger, then held it there while he met her gaze.

"This was my mother's wedding ring. The one my father gave her," he clarified, "not the one she wore when she was married to Jacob Bodean. After my mother passed away, I put the ring in my safe and that's where it has remained until this morning. Though it seems odd, now that I think about it, I never thought about giving it to my first wife. Maybe I somehow knew that it was meant for someone else. You."

He drew in a shuddery breath to steady his voice, then went on. "The love my parents felt for each other was strong, so strong that sometimes I was jealous of it. Mostly, though, I envied the relationship they shared. Especially after I became an adult. That's the kind of love I feel for you, Addy, the kind of relationship I want you and I to have. This ring symbolizes family for me, the love a man holds for his wife. Will you wear it as a physical reminder of my love for you?"

"Oh, Mack." She glanced down at the ring. "It's beautiful." When she looked up at him, her eyes were filled with tears. "I'd be honored to wear your mother's ring."

In her eyes he saw the same depth of love he'd seen in his mother's eyes when she'd looked at his father, the promise of a lifetime together. As he looked deeply into her eyes, he felt a distinct quiver in his heart, then a flood of warmth that spread slowly throughout his body, and knew it was a sign from the wife and son he'd lost, letting him know that they were glad that he'd found happiness again. At that moment he knew that his life had come full circle. An ending of one, a new beginning…and a son to carry on his family's legacy.

He pushed the ring all the way onto her finger, then raised her hand and pressed his lips to it, sealing the promise of his love. "I love you, Addy."

She lifted her face to his. "And I love you, Mack."

He kissed her deeply, wanting to show her with more than words the depth of his love. When he withdrew, he gripped her hand tightly in his. "I want more children. Sisters and brothers for Johnny Mack to grow up with."

She released a shuddery breath, then, laughing, threw her arms around his neck. "Me, too. I want that, too."

Hearing the crinkle of paper between them, frowning, Mack pushed her to arms' length and looked down. "What's that?"

She followed his gaze to the slight bulge in the pocket of her robe. "Oh, my gosh!" she cried and stuffed her hand into the pocket. "I forgot to tell you." She pulled out an envelope and held it up for him to see. "I found it! The piece of paper that my father sent my mother. It was inside the trunk, all along."

He took it from her to examine it. "This is from your father?" he asked, scanning the return address.

"No, it's from a soldier he served with. In fact, it's from the father of the woman who called and told me about the piece of paper."

He lifted his gaze to hers. "And…" he prodded.

She looked at him in confusion. "What?"

"Is it valuable?"

Taking the envelope from him, she slipped it back into the pocket of her robe and shook her head. "Not like you'd think." Smiling, she wrapped her arms around his neck again. "But to me it's worth millions."

* * * * *

A PIECE OF TEXAS *continues*
with Peggy Moreland's
THE TEXAN'S HONOR BOUND PROMISE,
available in
September from Silhouette Desire.

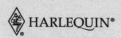

HARLEQUIN®

American ROMANCE®

American Beauties

SORORITY SISTERS, FRIENDS FOR LIFE

Michele Dunaway

THE MARRIAGE CAMPAIGN

Campaign fund-raiser Lisa Meyer has worked hard to be her own boss and will let nothing—especially romance—interfere with her success. To Mark Smith, Lisa is the perfect candidate for him to spend his life with. But if she lets herself fall for Mark, will she lose all she's worked for? Or will she have a future that's more than she's ever dreamed of?

On sale August 2006

Also watch for:

THE WEDDING SECRET
On sale December 2006

NINE MONTHS NOTICE
On sale April 2007

Available wherever Harlequin books are sold.

Join Sheri WhiteFeather in The Trueno Brides!

Don't miss the first book in the trilogy:

EXPECTING THUNDER'S BABY

Sheri WhiteFeather
(SD #1742)

Carrie Lipton had given Thunder Trueno her heart. But their marriage fell apart. Years later Thunder was back. A reckless night of passion gave them a second chance for a family, but would their past stand in the way of their future?

On sale August 2006 from Silhouette Desire!

Make sure to read the next installments in this captivating trilogy by Sheri WhiteFeather:

MARRIAGE OF REVENGE,
on sale September 2006

THE MORNING-AFTER PROPOSAL,
on sale October 2006!

*Available wherever books are sold,
including most bookstores, supermarkets,
discount stores and drugstores.*

Stability is highly overrated....

Dana Logan's world had always revolved around her children. Now they're all grown up and don't seem to need anything she's able to give them. Struggling to find her new identity, Dana realizes that it's about time for her to get "off her rocker" and begin a new life!

Off Her Rocker

by Jennifer Archer

HN53

Available August 2006
TheNextNovel.com

HARLEQUIN®
Next™

COMING NEXT MONTH

#1741 MARRIAGE TERMS—Barbara Dunlop
The Elliotts
Seducing his ex-wife was the perfect way to settle the score, until
the Elliott millionaire realized *he* was the one being seduced.

#1742 EXPECTING THUNDER'S BABY—
Sheri WhiteFeather
The Trueno Brides
A reckless affair leads to an unplanned pregnancy. But will they
take another chance on love?

#1743 THE BOUGHT-AND-PAID-FOR WIFE—
Bronwyn Jameson
Secret Lives of Society Wives
She'd been his father's trophy wife and was now a widow. How
could he dare make her his own?

#1744 BENDING TO THE BACHELOR'S WILL—
Emilie Rose
Trust Fund Affairs
She agreed to buy the wealthy tycoon at a charity bachelor auction
as a favor, never expecting she'd gain so much in the bargain.

#1745 IAN'S ULTIMATE GAMBLE—Brenda Jackson
He'll stop at nothing to protect his casino, even partaking in a
passionate escapade. But who will win this game of seduction?

#1746 BUNKING DOWN WITH THE BOSS—
Charlene Sands
A rich executive pretends to be a cowboy for the summer—and
finds himself falling for his beautiful lady boss.

SDCNM0706